CALLED BY A PANTHER

CALLED BY A PANTHER

A PANTHER

MICHAEL Z. LEWIN

THE MYSTERIOUS PRESS
New York · Tokyo · Sweden · Milan
Published by Warner Books

 A Time Warner Company

2322 0819

"The Panther" from *Verses from 1929 On* by Ogden Nash. Copyright © 1940 by Ogden Nash. First appeared in *The Saturday Evening Post*. By permission of Little, Brown & Co., Inc.

Mysterious Press books are published by
Warner Books, Inc., 666 Fifth Avenue, New York, NY 10103.

A Time Warner Company

The Mysterious Press name and logo are trademarks of Warner Books, Inc.

Printed in the United States of America
First Printing: June 1991

10 9 8 7 6 5 4 3 2 1

Library of Congress Cataloging-in-Publication Data

Lewin, Michael Z.
    Called by a panther / Michael Z. Lewin.
        p. cm.
    ISBN 0-89296-439-1
    I. Title.
    PS3552.E929C3 1991
    813'.54—dc20   90-84896
                                                            CIP

. . . if called by a panther,
Don't anther.

From "The Panther"
—Ogden Nash

You're never first;
you're never last;
you're just next.

—Lt. J. D. Jones, I.P.D.

CALLED BY A PANTHER

LORING, THE BUTLER, brought the bad news.

His timing was particularly poor as far as I was concerned. Parties like this always have a garrulous Brit and
tonight's was finally resting his mouth by using it to eat. That
had allowed the more interesting guests, like the Chief of
Police, to open up a bit.

The subject was terrorist bombs.

"In Indianapolis!" the hostess, Mrs. Vivien, had said.
"How could we ever imagine that terrorists would turn up
here?" She fiddled with the basic white pearls that hung
below the neckline of her basic black dress. She didn't sound
afraid, but I was pleased she was encouraging talk about the
subject rather than dismissing it as too, too boring.

"But they haven't managed to blow anything up yet, have
they, Chief?" the man on Mrs. Vivien's left said. "That's right,
isn't it?"

The Chief, no doubt, would have picked a happier
subject than the Scum Front given the choice. But he spoke
easily and said, "In fact, Dick, their first bomb was planted
and detonated in a cornfield out Lebanon way."

Mrs. Vivien laughed. "*Planted?* In a cornfield?"

I had had a sip of preprandial Scotch myself, so I said, "Do you think there is significance in the fact they picked the 'Lebanon' area, Chief?"

As he turned to me, his brow furrowed. Like a fallow cornfield. He said, "My bomb unit team just figures it was an easy place for them to get to."

"So do you think they're based on the northwest side of town?" Dick said. "That's pretty worrying for all of us who work out that way."

The Chief sipped from his water glass. "Course it could also mean that they aren't from the northwest and they're trying to put us off the scent."

Dick was a lawyer in his fifties with a leathery brown face and the build that I take to mean no matter what he drinks tonight, he'll be out jogging tomorrow morning.

I said, "I didn't realize that you had a bomb unit, Chief. Or has it been formed specially to cope with the Scummies?"

"Been around for years," he said. "Why do you think we've gone so long with so little of this kind of trouble?"

"Because there's nothing worth terrorizing?"

He fixed me with what a friend of mine in the force calls the Chief's baby-killer look. "Indianapolis may not be the first target for your average psycho terrorist, but that's no reason not to be alert. Specially as we get more and more big events here, the conventions and concerts, the Pan-Am Games . . ."

"Olympic track and field trials," Dick said, nodding vigorously.

"We're not just the Indy 500 town anymore. And please don't forget," the Chief said, "these pollution nuts may only have blown up a cornfield, but all five of the other bombs were left in big buildings and if any of them had gone off . . ." He looked at us in sequence, allowing time to think about the genuinely awful implications of explosions in *our* city. "But of course," he said, "we got to each one of them in time."

However, Mrs. Vivien looked up from her pearls to undercut the impact of the accomplishment. She said, "I thought the story on Channel 43 was that the explosive material in the last five bombs wasn't actually wired up." She looked to the Chief for confirmation but continued without it. "And don't they call Channel 43 each time, to tell where they left the bombs?"

I said, "If you've got to have bombers, I suppose ones whose bombs don't go off are the best kind."

But the Chief ignored me and turned to Mrs. Vivien. His smile was so broad and toothy and poisonous he could have been practicing to run for elective office. "Well, Charlotte," he said, "I know there's an element of the populace that doesn't take the Scum Front seriously because they claim to be fighting for wholesome things like pure water and because, *so far,* they've called in warnings. But if you think we ought to treat people who say, 'We *could* have blown the Hoosierdome to smithereens but we didn't,' as some kind of heroes or good guys, I believe you and me are going to have a falling-out."

"Now, Chief, you know I didn't mean *that,*" Charlotte Vivien said. But I never learned what she did mean, because that was when Loring came in with his bad news.

Still, he had his instructions, the butler. There is probably a protocol for this sort of thing, like bad news only between courses. Could be that, after training, butlers suffer not a moment's angst.

But me, my heart was pounding away. And it wasn't even love.

"Madam?"

"Oh," Mrs. Vivien said. "Yes, Loring? What is it?"

"Madam, I am distressed to have to inform you that Mr. Ripley . . ."

Loring took a breath. He was good. Everybody studied his face and waited for the air to come out again.

"Oh dear," Mrs. Vivien said. "Mr. Ripley." She looked down the table to the empty setting. "He didn't come through and I never noticed. Oh, what a terrible hostess I am!"

At the other end, the Brit laughed twice, a goosey kind of laugh.

"Be quiet, Quentin," Mrs. Vivien said.

Quentin sucked on a bread stick while most of us glanced toward the empty chair and untouched consommé and lobster parfait and tried to remember who wasn't sitting there.

And although this was a dinner party for twenty-two where nobody knew everybody and some of us knew nobody, everybody placed which one Ripley was: the loud drunk who had used the big F word about lawyers, who had been pulled off the Chief's lapels and who had kicked Mrs. Vivien's Siamese cat.

"Unfortunately, madam," Loring continued, "I have the distinctly unpleasant duty to inform you that at the present moment Mr. Ripley is lying behind the love seat in the drawing room."

"Good heavens," Mrs. Vivien said.

A murmur trotted around the table. Myself, I made no sound, but that's because I'm a tough guy and am experienced in the chicane of life.

"I regret, madam," Loring continued, stressing each word, "that there is a small ebony-handled dagger protruding from Mr. Ripley's chest and that there is a pool of what I presume to be blood on the small Turkish rug. I regret to inform you, madam, that Mr. Ripley has expired and that there is *prima facie* evidence of murder."

Response here was varied. A few intakes of breath, some wide eyes and the odd nervous smirk. I heard "golly" and "gosh."

Mrs. Vivien allowed herself an ember of a smile but before she could respond the Brit said, "Well, to paraphrase Noel Coward, if a murderer found Wilmer Ripley's heart with a knife, he, or she, must have had marvelously good aim."

Then a heavy man down the table, who wore the kind of gray suit that would cost me a year's rent if I was still paying rent, said to Mrs. Vivien, "Oh, very good, Charlotte. Very good."

Mrs. Vivien's smile burst into flame with this zephyr of approbation and she rose from her seat. She spoke to the butler but addressed the assembled company. "Well, Loring, I suppose we will all have to go into the drawing room and have a look at the body."

People looked first at each other.

Raising her voice to preempt premature movement, Mrs. Vivien said, "What very good luck that we just happen to have among us a *real private detective*. Everybody, may I introduce Mr. Albert Samson. Stand up please, Mr. Samson."

Slowly I stood to "oohs" and "aahs" and a few tentative claps of hand.

"Mr. Samson is that rarity and anachronism, a true-blue old-fashioned private eye, isn't that right, Mr. Samson?"

I gave one nod, the minimum.

"He has an office on Virginia Avenue near Fountain Square, above a luncheonette, and he has been following people on the mean streets of Indianapolis for years and years and years. I had advance warning that somebody at my party tonight might be in danger, so when I noticed one of his little ads in the *Star* I took the liberty of inviting Mr. Samson along just in case. Of course we also have our esteemed Chief of Police here tonight but he was invited strictly as a guest and because he is a friend, so I'm sure that he won't mind if, for once, we don't rely entirely on him."

A gracious smile from the hostess was traded for a gracious smile from Indianapolis's Chief of Police.

"So, if you will all follow Mr. Samson to the drawing room—being careful not to disturb any clues!—I believe Mr. Samson has brought along his fingerprinting kit and he is about to take the prints from the murder weapon. Not that I wish to tell you how to do your job, Mr. Samson."

She bestowed one of the smiles on me, for which I traded one of my own, along with two draft picks and a player to be named later. Her "gracious smiles" were a lot better than mine.

"After we've examined the scene of the crime, I'm sure we'll be able to get back to our meal while Mr. Samson makes further investigations, although it's quite possible that he will need to call each of us out of the room for an interrogative third degree. And please, while we're moving around, try not to get in the way of . . . Ben! Our cameraman!"

Mrs. Vivien turned to a tapestry screen in the corner of the dining room and from behind it emerged a tall man with a video camera resting on one shoulder and the bottom of a dangly earring resting on the other. "In the next couple of days," Mrs. Vivien said, "each household will be getting a copy of the tape."

News of this party favor was greeted with a chorus of surprise and approval from the guests as they realized they were present at and part of a special social occasion.

The plan, as scripted and rehearsed in the afternoon, was that Ben would stay with me while I analyzed the scene of the crime and collected evidence. Then, when the guests were back at the trough, I would call the diners out singly or in couples for very short interviews. I had been provided with supposedly telling, even risqué personal questions to ask each interrogatee. After dinner we would watch a replay of the interrogations together, solicit further questions and win prizes if we were acute enough to spot the right clues and deduce the solution which I would reveal. The prizes were various quantities of champagne. Oh, it was going to be one hell of a party.

And the low point of my life.

"All right?" Mrs. Vivien said. "After you, Mr. Samson."

2

WHEN YOU FINALLY DECIDE to try to sell your soul, the only way to do it is with enthusiasm, right? Am I right?

Or is that just another piece of bull-tonk like, say, "The easiest kind of lie to remember is the one that is true"?

Architects have mock-Georgian; *Chelonia* have mock-turtle; why shouldn't Samson have mock-profound?

I got home well after two, having been sustained only by the knowledge that time is one-dimensional and unidirectional and that all human events will end no matter how much one's intense misery makes them seem endless.

The butler was the murderer, by the way, in league with Quentin, the Brit. Quentin was in Indy as a "writer in residence" and it was he who had written the party scenario. He had been here more than four months, since the first of January. It was time for him to make a unidirectional move too.

* * *

Home was dark when I arrived. A timer switches my neon sign—"Albert Samson Private Investigator": snazzy, huh?—off at midnight. There were no lights in either Mom's or Norman's room.

When I got inside, I called my woman. "No matter what the time," she'd said. "As soon as you get home. I'm dying to know how it went."

"So how do you think it went?" I asked, as soon as she woke up enough to remember who I was.

"I'm sure you did wonderfully."

"It was distilled humiliation. The pure stuff. Sheer essence."

"But did the Vivien woman pay you?"

"Yes," I said, "she paid me."

"Well, that's terrific! It puts you weeks ahead on your financial projections."

"Yeah," I said, "in my new business as a performing sea lion. Great."

Just for the one evening. Name your price, Charlotte Vivien had said to me. I closed my eyes and dreamed and named a price. *It's a deal,* she'd said.

"It wasn't nearly enough," I said.

"Oh, come off it, Al," my sympathetic beloved said. "Stop moaning. Be . . . be anything! Relieved it's over. Angry at social inequality based on money. Filled with desire. Anything but sorry for yourself."

"I sneezed while I was applying the fingerprint dust. It went everywhere. Everybody laughed."

My woman giggled.

"I'm not joking," I said. "I really sneezed. Well, what can you expect? I've never taken a fingerprint in my life. Not for real."

"You should have practiced more."

"I should have practiced doing it bent down behind a couch—oh, excuse me, a love seat—with twenty people and a cameraman watching me."

She laughed again.

"Try to control yourself. Prove you're compassionate no matter what they say about social workers."

"I'll try," she said.

She failed.

"Your compassion is why I stay with you, you know."

"Why you stay with me? So why do I stay with you?"

"If you'd seen me tonight, you wouldn't."

"Don't you get a copy of the tape?"

"I told her not to make me one."

"I'll call her."

"Please don't," I said. Suddenly I was tired. "God. Suddenly I am exhausted."

"Good," she said. "That's good, Al." And then, "Come on now. Remember it was your idea to 'go for it.'"

I remembered. I said, "Yeah." I must have said it funny. The bitch laughed some more.

3

I AWOKE TO THE PHONE.

"I didn't wake you up, did I?" she asked.

"No. I'm still unconscious, so it's not a problem."

"I'm sorry I laughed at you last night."

"If you laughed, I guess it was because I was funny."

"Yup."

"At least it's over."

"And you got your money."

"This is true."

"That's *good*, Al."

"Is it?"

"Baby, even if the new regimen doesn't end up better, you'll have changed your problems."

"I know. I know."

"I've got to go cook now. I just wanted to say hello."

"Cook? As in food?"

"You can't come over, Al."

"I can't?"

"You're talking to Frank at three."

"Oh hell. Was that this year?"
"Good luck."

I held my face in my hands for a couple of minutes. Frank.

I found the *Sunday Star* inside the door that connects my rooms to the rest of the living quarters above the luncheonette. Mom must have brought it up before she went out for her Sunday Expedition. Its presence was recognizable as a gesture of support.

Bud's Dugout empties on a Sunday. Mom goes to anything, preferably something with a bit of spectacle. Because it was May she would be at the time trials for the 500 but at other times of year it could be a Colts game or even the Children's Museum—she likes the interactive exhibits. She used to frequent the zoo. But that was before that nasty male polar bear ate one of its cubs.

Norman, her twenty-year-old live-in tattooed rude inarticulate griddle man, uses his Sundays off to prowl. He might go out causing spectacle, for all I know, but I don't get along with him well enough to ask.

I made coffee and took the paper back to bed. It was full of the Scum Front because there had been yet another antipollution bomb. That made six. One a week. Each timed to make the Sunday paper. Seven including the one in the Lebanese cornfield.

The curious thing about it all was that the longer it went on, the more sympathetic the general public became to the "terrorists."

Oh, the idea of bombers in Indianapolis . . . That was awful. Terrifying. The people responsible had to be nuts and the longer it went on, the more frustrated they would become. It was only a matter of time, surely, before the bombs started getting wired up. Before they started going off. Before they started killing people.

It would end in grief. Had to.

But meanwhile the irreverence reflex that jerks whenever people are told the same thing too many times had led to a growing undercurrent of civic pride: *our* bombers didn't hurt anybody, got their message out and still hadn't been caught.

There was no diminishment in the massing of the forces of law and order, but meanwhile the bombers were hot. They were a sporting event. If there'd been someplace to go and watch, Mom would have been there.

This time the Scum Front had managed to leave their contribution in one of the "Pyramids"—three bizarre eleven-story office buildings up north.

How did they get one in there?

As before, a warning was issued and the bomb had been recovered without an explosion. Channel 43, "Environment TV," on the Cab-Co cable system had, again, been the vehicle by which information was given to the police.

From the timing to hit the Sunday papers, it was obvious that the Chief had already known about this week's bomb at the Saturday night party.

But I didn't read all the bomber stories. The psychological profiles, the speculation about Middle Eastern connections, the analyses of their "demands."

I had something else to read in this week's paper.

Finally I found it: *Dust off that family skeleton today. Albert Samson, Private Investigator.*

Appearing bare like that, boxed at the bottom of a page, it didn't look nearly as amusing to me as when I'd placed it.

Maybe the youthful Frank was right. Maybe my advertising campaign did need more pizzazz, more client targeting. More other stuff I couldn't remember.

And then there was a knock at the door.

But it couldn't be Frank, my woman's immature daughter's immature fiancé. The filmmaker. Who was making "industrials"—commercials to you and me—thereby learning his craft so he would be ready for his big break when Hollywood called.

Because it wasn't three yet. Was it?

The doorbell rang.

I did *not* feel like talking to Frank about the virtues and power of television advertising. Even if that was the way Go-for-It Detectives went for it on a Sunday afternoon.

Even if it did guarantee my woman some time alone with the headstrong daughter, time for her to deliver the latest barrage of "But Lucy's." "But Lucy, *marriage* has life-affecting implications that aren't immediately obvious . . ." "But Lucy, what's wrong with just shacking up with the guy for five or ten years first . . . ?"

Keep taking them pills, hon . . .

The bell rang again.

FRANK WAS BIG AND GAWKY and square-jawed and the worst thing about him was that he believed what he was saying.

He shook my hand like there was an off chance he could get oil to flow. He stared unblinkingly into my eyes. He exuded idiot competence and confidence. I could tell immediately why my woman hated him and why Lucy loved him. And green eyes. He had eyes that truly looked green. Or was that because of the money he hoped to make?

"Albert," he said, "I've been working really hard on your product concept. It's been a challenge, but I really feel that I can fill in the concept sink that your customer interface material is suffering from."

Oh dear, oh dear.

"I've got a number of options to present to you, but let me tell you now I think we really need to go in hard, so some of the suggestions I am going to make will exceed the initial budget concept you gave me. But it will really be worth it, it really will. I really want you to trust me on this one because it's really exciting me."

"Oh."

"Albert, you are at the cutting edge in your business. There simply aren't any other TV ads for private investigation services in Indianapolis at this point in time. The other agencies, large and small, are all taking passive profiles, so that opens the road to an aggressive attack, wide as the Grand Canyon."

"Oh."

"If we can establish your ads with distinctive image and flair, then you will have the opportunity to establish yourself as *the* brand name in your field in Indianapolis. Think about it. People won't say to themselves, 'I need a private detective.' They'll say, 'I need an Albert Samson.'"

"You want to make me into a Jello?"

"That's right! Isn't it great!"

Oh dear, oh dear.

But I had promised to give the kid some rope.

"That's an idea, Frank."

"It really is, isn't it? But it does mean, Albert, that you've got to get into television right away! In absolutely as big a way as you can afford. I know that as an undercapitalized service industry, you are likely to be reluctant to take on a large advertising commitment, but now is the time! Hock the family jewels. It will pay for itself in no time, I'm sure it will. I've mapped out a campaign for a series of short, interrelated commercials. Realistically I think we'll have to start with them on Cab-Co, because Cab-Co represents the best value in television advertising available in the city."

"You mean it's cheap."

"For television advertising, yes."

The kid obviously didn't value my jewels very highly.

"And it's offering some very good multichannel packages. Do you know much about Cab-Co?"

I hesitated.

Frank told me how Cab-Co was breaking the mold of the cable-TV business. How the fact that it had been given a franchise at all showed that it was something special. How to survive it had to compete aggressively and offer great deals to advertisers.

And there was a degree of logic to what Frank said.

Cable television in Indianapolis used to be doughnut-shaped. One company served the doughnut, another the hole. But suddenly local officials had eliminated the monopoly status of doughnut and hole and gave permission to a third company to compete throughout the complete pastry area.

When the new franchise was awarded it caused a stink, because another Indianapolis-based cable system operator, Omega, had made national news a few years before by trying in court to force the city to do exactly what it had now done of its own free will.

But Cab-Co won the new franchise because it had promised local programming and per-subscriber royalties far beyond levels that any other cable company would consider. Nobody in the trade believed that Cab-Co could survive, but operations began with a flourish in January. The subscriber jury of natural selection was still out, though Cab-Co's owner, Hershel Morgason—a Minnesotan who had married into a monied Indianapolis family—claimed loudly that he was "well on target."

"It's a special time for television in Indianapolis," Frank said. "You have chosen to make your big move at exactly the right moment. You really have."

"Ah," I said.

"Albert, do you even *know* the full range of services that you offer?"

"Well," I said.

"I've been drawing up a list of all the things that a private investigator can legitimately claim to make available to Napoleon and Josephine Public. And it's impressive, truly impressive."

He pulled a piece of paper out of his inside jacket and winked at me as he unfolded it. He began to read. "Security consultancy. Company background. Personnel evaluation. Litigation research. Insurance claims and fraud investigation. Surveillance. Executive and VIP personal protection. Creditworthiness. Political risk analysis. Accident reconstruction. Photography. Undercover operations. Missing persons investigations. Divorce research. Juvenile reconstructive work. Evidence acquisition for personal or court use. Theft recovery. Ballistics, voice prints, lie detection. Asset location. Electronic measures and countermeasures. Witness interviewing. Personal escort services. Adoption inquiries. Fraud, conspiracy and corruption investigation. Patent infringement investigation. Repossession. Courier service. Liquidation proceedings. Data control. Acquisition and merger research."

Frank put his list down. He smiled. He said, "Albert, you are *awesome!*"

I said nothing.

"The beauty part," Frank said, "is that you are a one-man operation. That's what's going to make selling you so easy. You are not anonymous and impersonal. When people call your number wanting to hire an Albert Samson, they're going to get through to Albert Samson! You don't even have a receptionist. People are going to be knocked out by that. You are the real article. All natural, no preservatives. You are a certified organic, no chemicals added, whole-food private eye and once we get started, nobody is going to want anything less."

"Oh yes?"

"What are you charging?"

I told him my new rates, established when I remodeled the rooms above the luncheonette and began to think of advertising. Rates that also allowed me to subcontract work, if I got too busy.

"Double them," he said.

Then he pulled out the storyboards he had prepared. Short spots, featuring me.

"Hang on, Frank. I don't know how to sell stuff on television."

"It's got to be you, Albert. You're the product!"

"But—"

"Look at this."

We looked.

"The commercial starts with an actor. He's middle-aged. He's overweight. He has five o'clock shadow. There he is, standing in front of an acre of used cars. He begins his spiel, about how he's going to *pay* people to take his cars away. While he's talking, we fade down what he's saying and at the same time we draw back and, look! *He's* on television! And then *you* walk on in front of the set and say, 'Would you buy a used car from this man?' You pause, to let the question sink in. Then you say, 'Let me find out if he's honest before you risk your money.' See, we've used the word 'honest' and people will associate that with you. Then we bring up your logo, name, address and phone."

"My logo?"

"And through the whole thing we are running a crawl that lists all the things you can do for people. We'll run that on the bottom of each commercial. It'll be magical!"

He stood back. He stared at me with those bright green eyes. He said, "Trust me, Albert. I know we can do it."

And for a moment, just a moment, I believed.

5

FRANK LEFT AT FOUR-THIRTY. I had commissioned him to draw up specific plans for a quintupled budget.

Well, I did have the Charlotte Vivien money.

But when he was gone I sat down at my desk and returned to the world I knew. I could hardly believe what I had done.

Yet wasn't the whole idea to end having to scratch for work, once and for all? And if I really made an effort to become a Go-for-It Detective, then maybe, just maybe . . .

The clock said I should be hungry, but I didn't feel like eating. I turned on the television: PBS, no commercials. I watched a cranky commentator argue that as carbon dioxide globally warmed the earth, people would need less heat in the winter, would therefore burn less fossil fuel and would therefore produce less carbon dioxide so in the end the balance would correct itself. So we didn't need to worry about it now after all.

I tried to heal.

He had just gotten to me when I was weak, Frank.

And I hadn't done anything irreversible.

And by occupying Frank I had given my woman a fair crack at the fair Lucy.

Persuasive broad, my woman.

Besides, she would probably approve of what I had done. We could go out, celebrate. Take in a movie.

My fantasies were interrupted. I heard footsteps on the stairs to the office.

I couldn't believe it at first.

Five-thirty. There was no reasonable explanation as to who it might be.

Yet one does not climb a flight of metal steps signposted "To the Detective" by mistake. Even the neon sign gets rested on the Sabbath.

Then the footsteps stopped. They rang my bell. The bell that is connected to the button below the brass plate that said, "Albert Samson, Private Investigator."

Not, surely, a client. No beleaguered Hoosier could expect aid or succor. Or security consultancy, personnel evaluation, litigation research, surveillance, VIP protection, political risk analysis or juvenile reconstructive work. Not on a Sunday.

You can't even get beer in Indiana on a Sunday.

Yet the evidence of a presence was irrefutable.

I answered the door.

Standing outside was a thin angular man with a shock of dark hair that half obscured his face. There was no obscuring the fact that it was Quentin, the party Brit.

I was too astonished to speak.

He wasn't. He said, "How was it for you?"

I stared at him.

"The party. Did you enjoy any of it?"

Since the party had been unspeakable, I said nothing.

"Look," he said, "sorry if you're not feeling jolly, but may I come in?"

"What do you want?"

"To hire you," he said.

"Hire me? What for?"

"I don't mean to be a nuisance, old chap, but it is rather important."

Oh well.

I stepped aside and he entered. In the middle of the room he shook his head so that for a moment he had the use of both eyes. He glanced around but then said to me, "I knew it when I saw you working so manfully through that awful murder script of mine."

"Knew what?"

"That you were someone I could talk to. A soulmate."

I waited, but it was not a good day for testing my patience.

"In England, you know, Albert is a name used by members of the working class and by princes."

"In Indiana, Albert is a name used by tired private detectives who don't like their Sundays interrupted. If you have something to say, please get on with it."

He laughed his goosey laugh. He punched me on the shoulder, man to man. "I have something to say," he said.

"Well?"

"I need you to help me murder my wife."

6

HE GRINNED AS I LOOKED at him. The expression was that of a pleased child.

"Out," I said.

"No, no! It's all right, it really is. It's nothing illegal."

And for the first time I felt a spark of interest. It kindled the Go-for-It Detective in me enough to ask, "You want to hire me, as in money?"

"Yes."

"American legal tender?"

He sat in my Client's Chair and hummed to himself.

The Go-for-It Detective unlocked his desk and found his organizer while he reflected on the "drunkard's walk" path that his life had followed to bring him to this moment. The Go-for-It Detective asked himself yet again whether money was really worth what it cost to earn it. But then the Go-for-It Detective thought about the face he would lose with his woman if he turned away a paying client without hearing him out.

I said, "You'd better explain what this is about."

"The first thing you have to understand is that I am a *poet*." Quentin rocked back in the chair and flopped his hair away from his face for a moment once again.

The accumulating stress got to me.

I said, "Name, I. M. A. Poet. Now, Mr. Poet, I understand that you want me to bump off a troublesome spouse. How would you like that done? Poison? Hanging? Bazooka? The real issue is whether you want her put out of her misery quickly or whether you want it to be long and agonizing. If the latter, perhaps I could recommend a death by natural causes because I can't think of anything that could make her suffer more than death by lingering marriage to a jerk-off like you."

Quentin leaned forward at this. The hair fell back over his face and I wondered if watching it would hypnotize me. "Please, Albert!" he said. "I need your help."

I waited.

"I am a poet," he said. "Not exactly honoured in my own land, but not a nobody. I also have a little inherited money. And as the proverb has it, money makes the mare go, so I have been able to devote myself fully to my art, provided I restrain any desire for personal luxury."

He squirmed to establish the luxury of greater comfort in the chair.

I said, "Go on."

"A year or so ago one of my verse collections fell into the hands of Mrs. Charlotte Vivien. Charlotte isn't sophisticated in the ways of poetry but she knows what she likes."

"And she liked your poems?"

"Happily, yes," he said.

"And?"

"Charlotte, as you undoubtedly know, is extremely wealthy in her widowhood and that allows her to indulge her fancies. She set the machinery going that brought me to Indianapolis. I am now entering the fifth month of an extended writer's residency. I do a few workshops, in libraries and high schools, but mostly I just write."

"That sounds pretty comfortable. So what's the problem?"

"My problem is that I have fallen in love."

This was not what I expected. I'd been thinking more in the territory of, say, gambling debts.

"To be in love!" He stretched his arms out and looked to the heavens. Well, to my ceiling. But he looked for the first time like poets are supposed to look. "That is the last thing I ever expected to say about an American woman."

"Who exactly are you in love with?"

"With Charlotte, of course. Wasn't it obvious last night?"

"Not to me."

"Ah, you were much too engrossed in the humiliating performance you had been engaged to give."

"I guess so."

"You did it beautifully, I thought. You gave off the most impressive aura of world-weary hackdom, the honest journeyman reduced to extreme expedients but retaining enough dignity not to sell out completely. They can buy my body but not my heart. I thought that your sneeze into the fingerprinting powder was a moment of minor genius. A brilliant piece of theatre which said, 'I may be a trained monkey but you can't make me do it your way.'"

I felt various things, but among them was surprise that he had applied so much attention to someone other than himself.

And then he said, "You are surprised I saw what you were going through, aren't you?"

In the circumstances I had to say "Yes."

"So you see, we *are* soulmates, you and I."

"And you have a wife you want murdered."

"Yes," he said. "And no."

I expelled a world-weary sigh.

"I've always felt that poetry needs freedom, so I have never actually contracted myself in matrimony."

"You want your wife murdered, but you've never been married?"

"Yes."

I said no words. My face might well have expressed something.

"Whenever I meet a new woman, I *tell* her that I am married. It keeps her from expecting too much."

"Oh."

"But never for a single moment did I consider that this Middle American fortress of self-righteous materialism would contain a woman so thoroughly captivating as Charlotte. I am completely and utterly taken. So I *want* to get married. I *need* to get married. Therefore I must shed my 'wife.'"

"O.K. You tell her you aren't married after all."

"No."

"Too simple?"

"Charlotte is well off. Vulgarly wealthy, in fact."

"Men have coped with marrying rich women before."

"Ah, but it's a problem for her. It affects the way she looks at men. Especially poorer ones. Like myself."

"Sounds a good, sensible Hoosier girl."

"So when I declare my love, Charlotte may have me investigated. She's done that before with men."

"I'm liking this gal better and better."

"Therefore, I need to be rid of my 'wife' in such a way that there is no risk that she will come back to haunt me."

"You are worried about being haunted by the ghost of a made-up wife?"

"I will devise a story to account for my wife's death. But I am not a storyteller. I am a poet. So what I need you for is to troubleshoot. I want you to analyze it from an investigator's point of view. To identify weaknesses from the perspective of how an investigator might work."

"But can't you just say your wife died suddenly and leave it at that?"

"I have decided," Quentin said, "to have her murdered."

"Why?"

"Because it will make Charlotte sorry for me."

"You want me to help make a fictitious murder so convincing it will fool the woman you love into being sorry enough to marry you?"

"I know it sounds pathetic," he said.

"I don't like it," I said.

"I'll pay you well." He took an envelope from his pocket.

"I brought you a retainer. Cash. That's how it's done, isn't it? So you can avoid paying tax on it. Is a thousand dollars enough?" He pushed the envelope across the desk to me.

"A thousand dollars? For something like this?"

"I know it's not nearly as much as you got for last night."

"I'm going to have to think about it."

"Well, why don't you keep the money until you decide. You can give it back if your scruples won't allow you to do the work. Less fifty, say, for your thinking time. Fair? Wait till you see exactly what I come up with."

I thought about it. My woman would say, "Fifty for nothing." I said, "All right."

"Wonderful."

"But we do the paperwork. And, for your information, I pay my taxes."

"It's a deal," he said. "And Albert, I'm sure you'll find no objection to what I ask of you in the end. I always know about things like that."

"You know shit, Poet," I said, in my head.

I took out my receipt book. I counted the money in the envelope. Twenty new fifty-dollar bills. I copied their serial numbers onto the receipt. "Now," I said, "your name."

"Quayle," he said,

"What?"

"Quentin Quayle. I have a middle name. Crispian."

"Your surname is Quayle? Like . . ."

"That's right."

"Are you related?"

"Not as far as I know, but it is a Manx name and I understand he has Manx antecedents."

"Manx?"

"From the Isle of Man. It's part of Great Britain."

"Oh."

"It's what first drew Charlotte's attention to my work. The name. The coincidence."

"Oh. Right." I made the receipt out to Quentin Crispian Quayle, took an address and phone number and sent him on his way.

MY WOMAN DIDN'T SEE the problem. "You don't owe Charlotte Vivien anything."

"I know."

"In fact, considering some of the things you said about her . . ."

"She's got a dumb idea of what makes a good party, that's all. I never said she was a bad person."

"But you do divorce work when you can get it, don't you?"

She knew I did.

"And you investigate for lawyers without needing to approve of their clients or sometimes without even knowing what kind of argument your work is supporting."

"Yeah," I said.

"So . . . ?"

"I just don't like the idea of being hired to deceive someone deliberately. Legal proceedings are adversarial and so are divorces. But one doesn't usually think about marriages that way."

"Your romanticism has always been part of your charm," she said.

"Oh, come on. You're not such a goddamn cynic about love."

"Love, no, but marriage, yes. Al, if the Vivien woman can't see through your friend Quentin's absurd manipulations, isn't it open season on her?"

"Soulmate."

"Excuse me?"

"Quentin is my soulmate, not my friend."

"Mmmm."

"I understand what you're saying, but while Quentin was talking I found myself feeling protective. The poor woman has so much money that she has to be suspicious of every man who smiles."

"If her money causes her so much grief, let her give it away. And if you want to protect somebody, how about muscling up for a deserving woman whose daughter absolutely refuses to benefit from her mother's painfully gained wisdom?"

I muscled up.

Sleep made me smarter. By the morning, Monday, I was ready to do whatever Poet wanted. I had a lot of years invested in the detective game. It was time to make them pay off. And I had to remember that I was going to have a hungry advertising budget to feed.

I telephoned one of the city's major detective agencies. Luckily I was able to make an afternoon appointment to see Graham Parkis, the agency boss. If I became even a tenth as busy as Frank said I would, I'd need to subcontract work. Therefore I needed to negotiate a standing arrangement with a larger agency now.

Parkis had done a great job for Frank's mother when she divorced his father. Found secret bank accounts and land and women and had left Frank's father a total wreck. So Frank recommended him. Not a sentimentalist, our Frank.

Then, about ten-fifteen, I got a call from a minion at a

downtown law firm. He said that one of the partners had been
at Charlotte Vivien's murder meal with his wife.

"Mr. Andrews says his wife thought you were cute," the
minion told me icily. "She wants her husband to use you.
That's if you do investigative work. Or are you just a guy who
does parties?"

I assured the minion that I was a working detective.

The minion asked my rates. I didn't follow Frank's instruction to double them, but as a gesture I added 25 percent. The
minion didn't bat an eardrum. He was empowered to offer me
a job immediately. It was a minuscule part of research for a
client who was considering a merger. I signed on, figuring it
would take about two days. The minion told me to appear at
the firm's offices at noon.

Pity I didn't remember which partygoer Mrs. Andrews
was.

But a Go-for-It Detective would find out. Get a copy of
the party video tape for reference. Right?

So I called Charlotte Vivien.

Loring answered. He took my name and went to ask Mrs.
Vivien if she was at home.

"Mr. Samson," Charlotte Vivien said. "How nice to hear
from you. I've had no end of people tell me they enjoyed your
contribution to my little evening."

"Oh. Well. Thanks."

"I know it was difficult for you, but I'm sure no one else
could have done it better," she said.

"I tried not to let them see how much I felt out of my
element."

"You handled the interviews particularly well."

"The novelty value was most of the battle. I don't think
your guests would have found it half so entertaining if they
were being interrogated for real."

"Of course not."

"But as a matter of fact the evening has led to two other
jobs."

"You mean my guests have hired you?"

"That's right."

"Heavens! Who?"

I laughed. "I can't tell you that, Mrs. Vivien."

She didn't see the joke. With force, she said, "Oh, surely you can tell me the names. It's not as if I had asked you whether they were divorce jobs."

"I'm sorry," I said. "I can't give you details of confidential cases. But neither is about a divorce."

"So you won't tell me?" This was a woman who was used to getting what she wanted.

"No," I said. "Look, I didn't call to get into an ethical dispute."

"What did you call for?"

"You kindly offered me a tape of the party. I declined it on the night, but if it is still possible, I've decided that I would like a copy after all."

"You had your chance," she said, and hung up.

So, maybe she and Poet deserved each other.

But I didn't get time to brood on the unexpected unpleasantness. Before I went out, the phone rang four more times. Two lawyers I had worked for in the past offered small jobs and two callers made appointments to talk about others. Not a single wrong number, wrong voice or heavy breather.

It was Monday morning, we hadn't done the TV commercials yet and I was already *hot*.

The daydream joyride with Frank was definitely on the agenda: "Get me an Albert Samson!"

A character actor named Jack Elam was interviewed on a TV program I saw once. He described the stages of an actor's career in Hollywood. There are six: 1. Who is Jack Elam? 2. Can we save money if we use, say, Jack Elam? 3. Get me Jack Elam! 4. I suppose we'll have to find the money for Jack Elam. 5. Get me a Jack Elam type. 6. Who is Jack Elam?

Maybe, just maybe, I was beginning to move from 1 to 2.

8

GRAHAM PARKIS WAS WAITING at the door when his secretary showed me in. We shook hands and I said, "Thanks for letting me come by at such short notice. I appreciate it."

"No problem, Samson. I always try to look out for other guys in the trade. We may compete for the money jobs using every known instrument of torture, but underneath the scabs and scars we've all got the same red runny stuff. It's a shit-hole way to make a living. Everybody hates you: the cops, the targets, even your clients. If we don't look out for the other guy a little bit, who can we turn to?"

"Uh, yeah."

"Make yourself at home," he said. He waved me into the room.

For a moment it was hard to tell where I was. Then I worked out that it must be an office because there was a computer terminal blinking on a walnut escritoire in a corner. Otherwise I would have guessed a Nevada whorehouse bar. It was that subtle.

"Care for a snifter?" Parkis asked. He pulled two tall

glasses from a gilt-edged shelf and then turned his back to open a small freezer.

"Not for me," I said. "Thanks."

Parkis drew out a white tub and flicked the top off. "Ice cream," he said.

"Oh."

"Teetotal myself, so I know where you're coming from. But ice cream's my tipple."

There was a spoon in the tub. He dropped two large clots into one of the glasses.

"Want some? Vanilla."

"No thanks."

He nodded, and put the ice cream back in the freezer. But before he returned to me he filled his glass with cola. The liquid fizzed around the colder ice cream. Parkis smiled broadly. "Called it a brown cow when I was a kid. Love it. What can I do for you, Samson?"

I explained that I wanted cover in case I became too busy to handle all my business myself.

"No problem about the personnel," he said. "I've got lots of guys and gals on standby for me. But what kind of money did you have in mind?"

I told him what I planned to charge.

"Oh dear," he said. He stirred his cow. "I suppose a few people would work down there." He thought some more. He decided to be generous to a red-runny-stuff brother. "Yeah. I can swing it. There's not going to be much left for you, of course."

"Oh."

"But I can see how you could look to go for the cheap end of the market hoping it will parlay into bigger things later on. Yeah, I can see that." He tasted the brown runny stuff in his glass and found it to his satisfaction.

Frank, in his pep talk, got his facts wrong. I may not have a receptionist, but when people call an Albert Samson they do not always get the man himself. Sometimes they get his machine.

That said, since I moved above the luncheonette I have a classy model. It takes long messages. I can debrief it by calling in. I can change my customer-interface content by phone.

Also it works.

Over the course of the week my answering machine earned its electrons by dealing with a string of calls including what turned out to be two more "now" jobs.

But there was no further contact from Poet. I didn't think a lot about it. Perhaps poets get writer's block when they're murdering fictional wives.

Somewhat more surprising, I did not hear from Frank. However, I was not moved to call him.

I was impressively, satisfyingly busy all week long.

But Saturday in the middle of the afternoon I was in my office again. My Time Management Flow Chart™ showed clearly that I was typing invoices, 3:15–3:35. In fact I was reading, a book. Just for a few minutes. Like I used to in the old days. Before I was a success.

And then my doorbell rang.

It surprised me. Not because I wasn't getting used to the little ways clients have of getting attention, but because I hadn't heard anyone come up the stairs. The stairs may be on the outside of the building, but they are metal and they make no concessions to noise pollution.

I put the book down and went to the door.

I found a young woman standing outside. "Yes?" I said.

She wore a brown coat which was ankle length but open enough in front for me to see sneakers.

"Are you . . . are you . . . ?" The voice, such as it was, came from under a floppy hat and from behind a threadbare mask of bright yellow hair.

"I are," I said. "Do you want to come in?"

She glanced away and by doing so drew my attention to a pale green station wagon parked in front of the gas station down the street. I couldn't tell if anybody was in it but I would have bet the young woman wasn't friendless.

"Uh, you're the detective, right?" she said.

"Right."

"Yeah, I'll come in."

The glance to the road had helped my visitor find her words. We went in and sat in the positions that befitted our respective roles.

My Client's Chair used to need dusting. Now I indulge in the fantasy that one day it might wear out.

It was hard to assess the age of my visitor at first. Twenty and tired? Thirty-five and in great shape?

"My name is Albert Samson."

"Uh, Kate King," she said.

"Can I help you in some way, Ms King?"

"It's a little complicated."

"I'm a little simple. That usually evens things out."

The idea, see, was to put her at her ease.

I had no visible success.

"Uh, look, I need to know, like, how confidentiality works with people like you. Uh, I don't mean people as people like you, but, like, detective-type people."

Oh.

"The laws of the state say that only you, as a client, may be given any information I obtain while I work for you. Is that what you mean?"

"Uh, yeah. Partly. But what, say, if somebody else, not your client, came to you and said, 'Hey, so and so that you're working for, tell me who they are and what they want.' What do you do when that happens?"

"I die with my lips sealed."

She studied me. "Is that serious?"

She was certainly serious.

I said, "The only time it doesn't apply is when criminal matters are involved. In that case the law says that I have an obligation to cooperate with the police."

"Oh," she said.

This was not a reassurance to her. She said, "And what about you? How do you decide when to go to the cops? Just as soon as there's a traffic ticket, do you go and pour it out to them or what?"

I decided she was twenty and tired.

"I don't involve the police unless I feel I have to," I said in as avuncular a tone as I could. "But nobody in my business can survive without reasonable relations with our friends in blue."

That didn't reassure her either.

I said, "You have some sort of problem, right?"

"Uh, I might have."

"And you think that I might be able to help you."

"Maybe."

"And would I be right to suspect you would have to be pretty desperate to bring me into it?"

"You can say that again."

In some company I might have. But not with Twenty, Tired and Humorless.

I said, "What I suggest is that you take the chance and tell me what's on your mind. Then I will tell you whether I think I can help. I won't take you for a ride. I won't charge you anything."

"Money's not a problem," she said.

Maybe in the whole world money is only a problem for me.

I said, "But before you say anything, let me try to give you a better idea about the sort of situation in which I would have to go to the police."

She said nothing and paid close attention.

I said, "If you told me that you had just murdered somebody, or had committed some other major crime—"

"I haven't murdered anybody," she said quickly.

"On the other hand, suppose you were worried that your boyfriend was a heroin addict. That wouldn't send me to the police, but if you told me that *he* had committed a murder, then it would. Does that help?"

"Not a lot."

"I am trying," I said.

"Yeah," she said. "I can see that," and the tone was for the first time, like the content, more personal.

"Well, maybe you can ask me something else that would help you decide."

"Suppose I was on the run for something."

"It would depend what the details were."

She sighed.

"I'm sorry if it's not getting clearer for you."

"Me too."

"You could begin to tell me what's wrong. I could stop you if you were getting into things I couldn't keep to myself."

But she had decided to leave. She stood up and said, "Maybe later."

"I hope you get some joy somewhere," I said.

She didn't indicate if she had heard. She marched to the door and left.

I sat for a few seconds, trying to hear her go down the stairs. But there was nothing. Maybe the wind blotted out what little sound she was making. Maybe tired twenty-year-old girls in sneakers just don't make much noise in this world.

I went to the window and saw my visitor get into the light green car down the street. She entered on the passenger side.

I waited, but it didn't drive away. I watched for three or four minutes.

Then I went back to my desk.

I put my book away.

I got out my invoices and began to work on them.

After a while I stopped. I was irritated that I hadn't maintained my observation post longer. I got up and looked out the window again.

The green wagon was no longer there.

9

KATE KING RETURNED AT seven-thirty. I was washing at my sink, getting ready to go out, when I heard the bell. It was Saturday night. I had a date and didn't want to be late. I answered the door shirtless, drying myself with a towel.

I said, "Oh, it's you."

She seemed struck dumb for a moment. The story of my life: a body that leaves women speechless.

Finally she said, sounding surprised, "You live here too?"

"Did you ring the bell thinking I wouldn't be here?"

"Uh, no. The light was on. I thought you were working."

"Did you want to come in?" I asked. "Or did you just stop back to tell me that I can't help you after all?"

It was out of hours. I was fabulously successful. I could afford to be just that tiny bit snotty.

Or was such a relaxation of mental attitude the first step along the path back to failure? Oh my God!

She said, "There's something I want you to do."

"Do? I thought you were deciding whether to tell me about a problem."

"Now there's something I want you to do."

"Come in and sit down. But give me a sec. Let me get dressed."

"O.K."

She came in.

I put on a shirt and fluffed my hairs and returned to the office. "So what do you want me to do, then?"

"Uh, deliver a package."

"What kind of package?"

"This kind." From a large pocket somewhere low inside her coat she produced a brick-shaped object, wrapped in brown paper and sealed with tape.

"What is in it?"

"Nothing dangerous."

A funny word to pick. I would have said, "Nothing illegal," if I had been trying to get me to do what she was trying to get me to do.

So I asked, "Something illegal?"

"Oh no. Nothing like that."

And for some reason—that person-to-person thing we all think we're so good at—I believed her.

"Where do you want me to take it?"

"To Garfield Park. Do you know where that is?"

On the south side of town. Not all that far away.

"Yes. And when I get there do I take ten steps northeast from the third willow tree on the left and whistle 'The Star-Spangled Banner' in the key of D-sharp major until a woman in a polka-dot bikini taps me on the shoulder and asks me what time it is in Tokyo?"

"What?"

"Ms King, this all sounds like spies and secret agents."

"No no. Nothing like that."

"How long is it going to take me to find something that it *is* like?"

"Just put it on one of the children's swings. The blue plastic ones near the main entrance. They're easy to find."

"And when do you want it done?"

"Now."

"Oh, now. Of course. Silly me."

"You'll do it?"

If she was aware that she was asking me to do something odd, she gave no hint of it.

Yet . . . I was getting curious.

Does a Go-for-It Detective get to be curious?

"I'm not sure," I said.

"We'll pay."

"We?"

"I mean I. I'll pay."

"How much?"

"How much do you charge?"

"For delivering packages to children's swings? The standard rate is a thousand dollars."

"Really?" She looked at me.

"No, not really," I said.

We were finally off her agenda, but she didn't know where we were.

I said, "I'll give you a choice of charges."

"Yeah . . . ?"

"If you tell me what this is all about, I'll do it for free. But if you don't tell me, it will cost you a hundred dollars."

"I'll take the hundred dollars," she said. Her free hand dived back inside the coat. It was there for a moment and then it came out with two small wads of bills. She didn't count them. How did she know I was going to ask for a multiple of fifty? Maybe she was a mind reader.

But she didn't push the money across the desk. She said, "There are conditions."

"Oh. Conditions. Right. And what might those be?"

"Under no circumstances are you to open the package, number one."

"Don't open package," I said. "Right."

"You are to leave within ten minutes after I go."

"Leave within ten minutes, right."

"And you are to follow the specific route I tell you. South on Shelby Street till you pick up 431. Leave 431 on Southern. The park is on the left."

"Predetermined route." I waited. "Is that all?"

"Yes."

"Now I'll tell you my conditions."

"Your conditions?" The idea hadn't crossed her mind. "What do you mean?"

"Number one, you and I will go downstairs where you will meet my mother and her boarder, Norman."

"What?"

"In front of my mother and Norman you will state that nothing in or about the package is illegal in any way whatever."

She narrowed her eyes. "Yeah?"

"Then you will give me the hundred dollars. And I will give you a receipt. Those are my conditions. I'm sure you will agree that they are no more than simple protection for me."

She was silent while she wrapped her mind around what I had said.

"Do you agree to my conditions?"

"Uh . . . uh, I don't know."

"Maybe you'd like some time to think. Maybe you'd like to step outside while you do it."

"Yeah. Yeah, I think I'd like to go outside and think about it."

"That's fine."

I let her out.

This time I stood by the closed door as she descended and I did hear a few footfalls. Just a quiet kid, I guess.

I moved to the window and from it I watched her cross the street to a station wagon parked on the other side. This time she got into the back seat. The car was parked well away from lights and I couldn't tell what color it was. But I was willing to make a modest wager that the light of day would have revealed it to be pale green.

Or is gambling the way successful people became unsuccessful again? This damn life is so full of traps.

When the car my would-be client got into did not immediately drive away, I left my lookout and phoned my woman to tell her I was probably going to be late.

"You have a client?" she said. "Oh, don't give me that! If you're going to make excuses, make it something believable."

Quite a wag, my woman.

KATE KING REAPPEARED at the door after twenty-five minutes.

"Long time no see," I said.

"I accept your conditions," she said.

"O.K."

She came in and without further niceties, I led her through my quarters to the inside stairs. We went down to the living room where Mom and Norman were playing Scrabble.

"Mom. Norman. May I introduce Ms Kate King. Kate King, this is my mother, Posie Samson, and Norman Tubbs."

Mom said, "How do you do?"

Norman looked up as if we were q's without u's.

Kate King shifted her weight as she stood but said, "How do you do?" So I knew she was well brought up.

"What can we do for you?" Mom asked.

I said, "Ms King is hiring me to deliver a package for her. Show them the package, if you would, Ms King."

She pulled out the brick.

"Ms King has declined to tell me what is in the package

but assures me that nothing whatever about it is illegal. I would like you to witness her telling me that. O.K.?"

Mom said, "Good heavens. What are you playing at, child?"

Norman played a four-letter word.

Kate King turned to me. "What do I say?"

"Tell me that nothing about the package is illegal."

"Nothing about the package is illegal."

"Hand on heart?"

"Hand on heart."

"Got that?"

"Yes," Mom said. Norman concentrated on feeling the letters in the bag before he drew any.

"Ms King is now going to give me an amount of money and I am going to give her a receipt. The money is for delivering the package and for nothing else. Right, Ms King?"

"Right."

"The money, please."

She produced the money again. After a count, I wrote the receipt.

We returned to my office.

"I will set off within ten minutes after you leave," I said.

But she didn't head straight for the door. She was silent for a moment and then she said, "I never thought about you with a mother."

I smiled, the smile I smile when young people say things that are young. But inside I was sad because whatever trouble this young woman was in, I was ready to bet my success that it was deep and unfragrant.

"I like her," Kate King said.

"I like her too," I said. "Why don't you come back and see her sometime?"

"I don't know about that," she said.

"She cooks a mean hamburger down there. Got meat in it even," I said, trying to find a contact point.

But I missed by a generation. "Oooh, dead animals!" Kate King wrinkled her nose.

She left.

Either my mother's hearing is more acute than mine or

she'd been watching the bottom of my stairs because within seconds of Kate King's departure Mom was in my office. I was putting on my coat.

"I'm glad you came up," I said. "I was about to come down to you."

"Who was that girl, Albert?" Mom asked.

"You know more or less all that I know."

"Why was she wearing that funny wig?"

"Wig?"

"Oh, you must have noticed she was wearing a wig. And a cheap one at that."

"I just thought it was one of those things that kids do to their hair these days."

"For heaven's sake, Albert!"

"I may need to hire an observant assistant soon. You ever thought about coming into the business with me?"

"Delivering funny packages? What kind of business is that?"

"Give it some thought, Mom. Let's do lunch."

She despaired.

I said, "Can you do something for me?"

"What?"

I took out the packaged brick. "Cut the paper on the end and have a look what's in there."

She squinted at me. "Why don't you do it?"

"I promised I wouldn't open it."

"Oh, honestly!" she said. But she took the package and I got her a sharp knife.

She slit the brown paper cleanly along the top of one end of the brick, then down one side to make a triangular flap. She folded the flap back and took the brick over to a light.

"What's the verdict?" I said as I found clear tape to stick the brown paper back together with. The tape would be hard to see in the dark.

"There might be something else inside," she said, "but all I can see is cut-up pieces of newspaper."

DIPLOMATS FROM "UNFRIENDLY" countries are followed routinely when they leave their embassies. They know they are being followed. And the people following them know they know.

Sometimes a "diplomat" wishing to show bravado rather than diplomacy goes to a follower waiting in a car and taps on the window and tells the follower where he's going next: "In case traffic gets heavy and you lose me."

As I drove off to Garfield Park and passed the parked presumably-pale-green car, I was tempted to stop. "Just in case your battery's flat and you need a jump start." It was even more tempting because the car seemed to be empty.

I had a vision of two, three, four? people piled on the floor. But much as I would have enjoyed looking down at my clients in their distress, I drove on.

Temptation: another trap for the Go-for-It Detective. If I stopped for a peek I might kill my chances for repeat work. There were literally thousands of children's swings in Indianapolis. At a hundred bucks a time I could retire on delivering newspaper bricks alone.

I drove to the park. I dropped the package into one of the swings and looped back to my car without breaking stride. I got in and drove away. Job done, conditions met.

Work finished: let play begin!

"We'll stay in," my woman had said. "We'll try something we've never done before."

I drove methodically to my woman's house. I spent as much time looking in the mirror as through the windshield. I made squealing television-type turns without signaling. I timed some lights so that I was the last car through on the yellow.

I am not a surveillance specialist, but unless the Kate King Gang's driver was, I had not been followed.

Once I was sure of that, I considered contacting the police. Well, not the police exactly, but my friend—now a captain—Jerry Miller. But what would I tell him? A funny-looking girl hired me to do deliver some waste paper. She had a friend with a station wagon. She paid cash.

In the plastic society, the cash was maybe the most suspicious part.

It was not the stuff of interrupting a friend's Saturday night.

And it wasn't as if I was really worried.

I should have been.

Waiting at my woman's were a battery of lights, a big video camera on a spidery base and boxes of sound equipment.

Also Frank. "Sorry I didn't get back to you directly, Albert," he said. "But I've got this big project in the air." He winked. "Can't talk about it now."

A small mercy and the only one I got all evening. We filmed my bits for a series of commercials.

If I'd known! I could have had my hair done. I could have bought a new frock.

* * *

"Please don't be angry at me," my woman said later. "They came to dinner on Wednesday and Frank talked ceaselessly about the plans he had for you and your commercials and how wonderful you would be on them if only you were relaxed and yourself. I said I'd like to see you do them and one thing led to another and tonight seemed about the only time we were all going to be free."

"Oh."

"And we felt that you would be more spontaneous if you hadn't spent a lot of time worrying."

"We did, did we?"

"Honestly, you *did* do well, Al. I was tremendously impressed. You came across beautifully. I can see you might resent the way it was done, but the result was really very, very good. A lot will depend on what material Frank super-imposes you onto, but your bit will bring you love letters and indecent proposals. Honest."

"Promise?" I said.

"You like that idea?"

"You know how it goes," I said. "Life moves on. One becomes successful. The friends who served so well just don't seem to understand one's new problems."

"Ah. I see. You don't like my collusion."

"I admit to being not real happy. I was in a good enough mood when I got here, but these carryings-on have not been dignified. No, I'm not real happy now."

"I don't believe you," she said.

"You don't?"

"I think you're pleased with how it went and that nothing would please you more than if this advertising makes your business boom. I think you're just affecting a bad mood."

"So, under this sensitive world-weary exterior there beats a heart that wants to become private detecting's Jello?"

"Yes."

"You're right. I am affecting a bad mood. I am affecting it very well."

"Is there anything I can do about it?"

"Yeah."

"You going to tell me?"

I raised one eyebrow, like I had on one of the commercials. It's what I do when I try to elicit love letters and indecent proposals.

But then I said, "Hey, what's this about dinner on Wednesday? You sat at the table with Frank? Do I gather that you are more resigned to having it as a son-in-law?"

"Over my dead body."

"I see," I said. "You're softening."

AND THEN THE *SUNDAY STAR* was without its where-we-found-the-bomb story. "Is it over at last?" the *Star* asked. Maybe the media-led "vigilance" was beginning to have an effect.

Or maybe there had just been a glitch in Scum Front dynamite deliveries.

Tune in next week.

Instead I read an extended progress report about a different kind of terrorism. The kind that has lots of money and knows all the right people and gets pats on the back in the editorial columns.

The report was on the progress of the urban mall over Washington Street, with its "skyways" to protect urban shoppers from urban traffic and urban weather while they used their urban credit cards and traded urban gossip.

There were problems. Frontline stores were hesitating. Though holes had been blasted, work was stalled. Oh dear. What a pity.

Washington Street. The old U.S. 40. Washington, D.C., to

Indy and points west. Now to be the basement for a giant-
sized Hamster World?

Or was I just sour because my career as a success hadn't
turned me into an urban spendthrift yet?

After lunch I applied myself to invoices, in preference to
Lesson Twelve in *Teach Yourself Bookkeeping*. I drank
orange juice. I mused on whether my new dynamic life was
going to be punctuated by humiliations every Saturday night.

Five-fifteen. My doorbell rang. It was my soulmate.

"Poet," I said at the door, "did I mention that I charge
double rates on Sundays?"

I made way for him to come in. He went straight for the
Client's Chair and dropped onto it. He made a winded sound.
"Sorry about interrupting your devotions, old man, but op-
portunity has knocked and needs to be answered."

I moved to my Go-for-It Detective desk. "Well, I've
decided that I will do what I can to help you, within reason."

"That is a great relief to me." He stared intently. "Thank
you," he said.

"So what's happened?"

"Tomorrow must be the deadly day. Tomorrow I do the
deed."

"What's special about tomorrow?"

"Both Charlotte's children have been home from college
all weekend and they each brought friends."

"I don't understand."

"Suddenly Charlotte is distraught and upset. She may
say she loves a high-activity, high-intensity life, but she
seems to have lost control. And I can't fault her. There is no
one on earth who could keep control of seven self-indulgent,
narcissistic, hyperactive American college students on a
manic party weekend. It is time to strike!"

"Oh."

"Well, tomorrow morning it shall be. I'll console her over
breakfast. I'll remind her what responsible people they will

become, despite being boors at present. I will amuse her with quotes from Shaw and Wilde and Dorothy Parker. 'She speaks eighteen languages and can't say "No" in any of them.' Do you know that one?"

He paused, but it wasn't a real question. He said, "And then the telephone will ring and it will be for me. 'Who can it be?' I shall ask when Loring brings the extension to the breakfast nook. I shall look worried for a moment. But I shall say, wittily, 'Probably the Nobel Prize Committee, saying I'm to get Literature.' She will laugh, my Charlotte, and I will say, tentatively, 'Hello?' "

I watched him mime the phone call, rehearse his facial expression.

"And, lo and behold, the caller will be Vanessa's mother! She will tell me that Vanessa—"

"Who is Vanessa?"

"My dear departed wife. So rudely and untimely murdered. Struck down in the prime cut of her maturity by a gang of yobbos on the prowl."

"A gang of what?"

"Ruffians."

"Ah. Ruffians. Poet, just how are you going to arrange to be called transatlantically?"

"Oh, that's all in hand, dear boy. I have a sister. She's a bit of a thespian. I dictated the text to her last night. She's going to ring in the morning, our time. I've told her when Charlotte and I will be at breakfast."

"You live at Charlotte's?"

"No no. I have an apartment as part of my residency. But I will twist my ankle tonight and ask to stay over. Charlotte will agree, but be slightly suspicious. But I shall make not a single suggestion or comment with innuendo, the perfect gentleman. We shall be perfect pals."

"Well, I guess you've got it all worked out. So does that mean you don't need me after all?"

But that was not what he meant.

*　*　*

He went through the story he had worked out for Vanessa's fate. It was strong on scene-setting and emotion and the injustice of random violence. It also had a moral: anything good in life must be grasped because life is all too short.

My "job," when he finished, was to comment.

"As if you had been hired to investigate events," he said, tossing his hair. "What would you do? Where would the holes be?"

"The problem, Poet, is that if anybody questions the facts at all, the result will be to find that the entire thing is a hole."

"What do you mean?"

"Suppose somebody asked me to check. The first thing I would do is telephone the police where the murder was supposed to have happened. And I would ask for the officer in charge of the Vanessa Quayle murder. And they would say 'Take a hike' or whatever police say over there when someone asks about a murder they've never heard of. And that, Poet, would be that."

"Surely they wouldn't talk to you on the telephone."

"They would tell me that they had never heard of a murder victim named Vanessa Quayle."

He cogitated. He said, "I won't specify where it took place."

I shook my head. "If anybody suspects it's a phony, all it would need is the I.Q. of a jogger to crack it in a day."

He sniffed a couple of times. But then he said, "You're the expert. What do you recommend?"

"Am I allowed 'Forget it?'"

"No," he said. He slipped his right hand under his shirt and flapped it. It represented his fluttering heart.

"Your only chance is if nobody asks, 'Is this story true?'"

"Mmmm."

"So flood your audience with details. Have your sister get a printer to prepare a newspaper clipping. Arrange to get phone calls of condolence. Letters from lawyers about your wife's estate. Everything like that you can think of."

"I see."

"Are you going to the funeral?"

"Absolutely not. The funeral's already taken place.

Vanessa's mother will tell me that tomorrow and I will be upset because I would have flown back. Charlotte will console me."

"O.K., then arrange to get a telegram about funeral expenses. A fax from your wife's executor asking if Aunt Edna can have the crocheted bedspread she loved so much."

"I see," he said.

"Ask advice from people here. Shall I help her relatives? Keep the game on your territory. It's your only chance."

He nodded vigorously. "That's great, Albert. You've given me some good things to think about."

"All part of the service," I said. I thought about adding a new entry to my "awesome" list. If I could find a way to describe it.

My client rose. "I'm going to go home and make some plans."

And little as I had wanted him to disturb my Sunday, I had trouble settling again once he went. I still didn't like the idea of what he was doing. But I didn't much care for the idea of doing more bookkeeping either. Especially while the sun was still shining.

NIGHT SEEMED TO FALL with a thud. Right on the back of my neck. Being alive became uncomfortable. There was nothing I wanted to do. The last thing in the world I wanted to be was a Go-for-It Detective. Or any kind of detective. Or even a major-league pitcher: it was that bad.

I hate it when I have gut feelings and can't sort them out.

I want to wave a wand and stop time and be presented with a set of life footnotes.

But it never happens.

Time limped on, and after twenty profoundly uneasy minutes I finally did a constructive thing: I wrote a list of the things I didn't want to do.

Then I decided to write my daughter a letter.

I got out a piece of paper. I filled my fountain pen.

But I didn't start it. Instead I sat and doodled and wondered where she was. I didn't know, except that when she and her sculptor parted, she left France and was some- where else in Europe. I could write to Switzerland where her mother had lived since . . . Since forever. Since marrying her fancy husband, having shed the original plain one.

Daughters. What was she doing? I knew she had taken to hanging around with some highbrow musicians. Was she involved with a musical Frank? How could one explain to a woman in her early twenties what was wrong with a Frank? Apparently acceptable, by the standards of society. But not a person to trust something precious to.

Like so many men, his bottom line read, "How was it for me?"

Pointless, pointless, pointless ruminating.

I hit myself in the head. Doing what a just God would do, if he or she existed. Saving him or her the effort if he or she didn't.

What kind of value can you give to the opinion of someone who just nods and smiles when he gets called "soulmate" by a Quentin Crispian Quayle?

I took a coffee cup and threw it at the door. Because it's the kind of thing that I never do.

The cup broke, of course. I looked at the pieces on the floor. I began to count them. I played a game. How many could I see without getting up from my chair? But what constituted staying in my chair, my "Detective's Chair"?

First I sat still with my elbows on the desk. Then I stretched as far as I could to right and left. Then I drew my feet up and stood on the seat.

Then I sat down again and, carefully, tipped the chair over while doing my best to maintain fundamental contact.

Once sprawled on the floor, I began to laugh and laugh and laugh and become wholer again.

And then, to punish my return to non-wand-waving humanity, I heard heavy footsteps on the outside stairs.

The doorbell rang.

14

OUTSIDE WAS NORMAN, the lodger thing.

"I lost my key," he said. "Can I come through?"

Norman had never been at my door or in my office before. I said, "How did you lose your key?"

He didn't answer me. He slipped past me and crushed pieces of coffee cup.

But in my bedroom he stopped after opening the door which connected me to the rest of the house. He said, "I've been meaning to have a word about your mother."

Him? Talk to *me* about Mom?

He said, "I think you're taking advantage of her, using this place like you do."

"I'm taking advantage? Compared to you, I—"

But he was gone and pulled the door closed behind him.

And then the doorbell rang again.

I couldn't believe it.

"God," I said, addressing It directly. "I saved you some time and effort a few minutes ago. Is this gratitude? Whatever happened to Sunday as the day of rest, huh? You getting senile or something?"

At my door was Kate King.

Her cheap wig still covered most of her face.

"Yeah?" I said.

"Uh, well . . ." She glanced at a part of the porch I could not see. Then she said, "You didn't follow the instructions."

"Yes I did. *I* didn't open the package. My mother opened it for me. You should be more exact about your language in the future, if you're so goddamned fussy."

She stood frowning and uncertain.

I knew she was somebody's daughter but I didn't care. "Sorry," I said. "No refunds."

"Uh, can you give me a minute?"

"I could give you a whole goddamned lifetime, lady." I closed the door in her face.

I walked back to my chair.

I sat down.

And I heard people talking, female voices. The tones were those of whispered dispute. I couldn't hear the words.

Adrenaline began to clear my self-indulgent mind.

I stood. I took a step toward the door.

But I stopped and returned to my desk. I sat and opened the drawer I keep my cassette recorder in. I loaded it with a blank and plugged in the concealed microphone that Go-for-It Detectives sometimes find useful when there are no independent witnesses to conversations.

There was no guarantee that the women outside my door were debating anything more than which park to leave the next newspaper brick in. But it was odd enough for me to be cautious.

The voices stopped. My bell rang again. I went to the door.

Kate King stood in front of three figures in long hooded jackets.

Each of the three also wore an animal mask.

"Oh, terrific," I said. "A breakout from the zoo?"

"Please!" Kate King said. "This is important. Let us in."

I shrugged. And stood back.

The Animals came in three species. First was the Frog. She was about five feet tall and wore sneakers.

She stepped on some cup shards. She stopped and, in a squeaky high voice, asked, "What's the stuff on the floor?"

"We have a lot of trouble with barefoot burglars in this neighborhood."

Behind her came a Bear and behind the Bear a Gorilla. They all wore sneakers, and now I saw jeans at the bottom of the jackets. The Bear was maybe five four and the Gorilla five eight.

They stepped carefully and the Gorilla closed the door behind them.

For a moment everybody stood without speaking. I said, "So when do I find out what the hell is going on?"

The others looked at the Frog. Maintaining her artificially high voice she said, "I have been elected spokesperson."

"O.K., Spokesperson, sit your asylum escapees on the bench next to the door."

She nodded. The others sat.

I pointed her to the Client's Chair and I went behind my desk.

The Frog and I sat facing each other.

The Frog took a breath and said, "We are the Scum Front."

"I DON'T BELIEVE THIS IS happening to me," I said. "Top of the all-time Indianapolis Most Wanted List, and they stroll into my office."

"We haven't come here to give ourselves up," the Frog said.

I looked across the room to the Bear and the Gorilla. At Kate King's mask of artificial hair. "No, I can see that." I hadn't heard any speculation that the Scum Front was a gang of women. My mind was racing. They weren't here to plant a bomb in my mother's luncheonette.

I looked at the Frog's hands. On four fingers there were white stripes near the knuckle. Whoever she was, she lived a tanned enough life to have ring lines in May.

"So what the hell *is* this about?" I asked.

"We have a problem," the Frog said.

I nodded. I said, "I take it Ms King has explained my position about knowledge of criminal acts."

"We don't think of ourselves as criminals," the Frog said.

"The definitions I have to respond to come from the police."

"Oh, we know that there's a chance that you'll run straight to the cops. But I believe you'll see you have a higher obligation than that to so-called society's law."

"Oh," I said.

"We have a problem," she said again. "We are too vulnerable to solve it ourselves. And maybe we shouldn't do anything about it at all."

She looked to her colleagues on the bench. They sat rigidly, watching us, listening.

And I recognized that it must have been a traumatic process to decide to reveal themselves after remaining utterly anonymous for so many weeks.

It meant their problem was important.

The Frog said, "We settled on taking one person into our confidence. There is no time to spare, but if you decide not to help, that's all we'll do. Mr. Samson, you are—genuinely— the only person who can prevent a tragedy."

"I think you'd better tell me what's going on," I said.

"They call us terrorists," the Frog said, "and in a way of course we are. But the only terror we seek to inspire is in those people whose lust for 'possessions,' and 'property,' and 'material development' is destroying the real, living world that we and future generations must live in. If somebody doesn't stop them, they will destroy us all."

"Please don't give me a sales pitch. I have some sympathy with your goals, but I have no sympathy whatever with bombs, even if they don't explode."

"Not just bombs that don't explode," she said. "Bombs that *cannot* explode. If we are terrorists, then at least we are socially responsible terrorists."

I said nothing.

"Look at our record," she said. "We've destroyed nothing, yet we have made a major impact on the media and therefore on public awareness. They know that there finally is a group in Indianapolis dedicated to protecting—"

I held up my hand. "My tolerance for political lectures is extremely limited."

"Well, how would you change what's happening in this

city, then?" she asked. "Education? The democratic process?"

"I suppose."

"But the people with the power have those things tied up
so tight—"

"You don't have to convince me that society is heavily
biased toward the haves at the expense of the have-nots."

"So the logical extension is clearly to formulate alterna-
tive—"

"Stop," I said.

"But—"

"Stop. My limit has been exceeded."

She stopped.

We all took some breaths in silence.

"I was trying to explain our thinking," she said.

"I'm thunk out," I said. "You claim there is danger of a
'tragedy.' Get on with it or get out."

"We left a 'bomb' in the Merchants Bank Building on
Friday."

But there'd been nothing in the paper. I said nothing.

"We made a warning call in the early hours of Saturday
morning. We call a cable television company—"

"Cab-Co's Channel 43. I know."

"Do you see our messages?"

"No. But I have a friend who follows you guys closely
and when we go out to lunch he tells me what you've been up
to."

"Public awareness," the Frog said, scoring her point.

No point in mentioning that my friend is a cop.

"When we call Cab-Co," the Frog said, "we give a code
word, so that they know for sure it's us. So Saturday morning
we made our call. Cab-Co contacted the police. The police
went to the building and they looked where we told them to.
Everything as usual."

"And?"

"The bomb was not there, Mr. Samson."

"What do you mean, not there?"

"I mean that between the time we left it and the time the
police got there somebody took it."

"Still, if it can't go off . . ."

But as I spoke I realized what the problem was. "Oh," I said. "The instructions."

The Frog nodded.

The point of a Scum Front bomb was to say, "Look! We *could* have blown this place up *if* we'd wanted to." To imply that next time they might, if they didn't get what they demanded.

But just leaving a bag with a few sticks of dynamite didn't prove that they could have set the bomb off. An explosion needed a detonator and a timing device. And the knowledge of how to put them together. So Scum Front "bombs" included a wiring diagram.

I said, "That means someone is walking around with a bomb kit."

"HOW EASY WAS THIS BOMB to find?"

"Not easy at all," the Frog said.

"And do you have any idea who's got it?"

"No."

"How did you find out that the police didn't recover it?"

"When there was no news report, we called Cab-Co again and the man we talk to there said the police hadn't found anything."

"Who do you talk to there?"

"The front man for the environmental channel."

"How come he hasn't told the cops you're women?"

She sighed with impatience. "Is that important?" Then, "We use a computer voice distorter, tape what we have to say and then play it into the phone."

"Oh."

"We have planned this campaign very carefully, Mr. Samson."

"But you never considered the possibility that one day somebody might pick up one of your bomb kits?"

"No," the Frog said. "We just didn't think of it."

Well, at least no excuses.

I looked at the bench again. Kate King and the Animals continued to watch impassively. Considering the tone of dispute I'd heard through the door before they came in, the discipline of the group was impressive. But that was what clandestine organizations were supposed to be like, wasn't it? Charismatic leadership and an emotional cause. Flawed individuals subjugating their individuality to external goals.

I looked at the Frog. She was articulate. But charismatic?

At least she wasn't an uncontrolled loony. Once we got past preliminaries, she had responded to what I asked.

"And you want me to try to find your bomb?"

"We want to hire you. We intend to pay."

"But how the hell am I supposed to find it?"

"If you agree to try you will have information that the police could never get. We've reconstructed what happened from the time we chose the Merchants Bank till our phone call. We can provide you with details that might give you a lead."

"Such as?"

"I can't begin to talk about that without an absolute assurance from you that you will *not* involve the police. That you will *not* tell them anything that you learn about us."

"How can you ask that of me? An 'absolute' assurance?"

The Frog said, "If we get the slightest indication that you have told the police what you know, we will stop helping."

I rested my chin on my hands and considered. "You put me," I said, "in a very difficult position. You are asking me to risk the license that my entire livelihood is based on."

"We're asking you to try to prevent loss of life."

"And all the malarkey about the package to be delivered to the swing in the park?"

"Improvising a way to see whether you would follow instructions."

"Why me?"

"Excuse me?"

"Why have you come to *me*?"

"Because," the Frog said, "you work by yourself. We decided to risk telling one person. Only one."

"You people have already given me more information about yourselves than the police have. How can I avoid telling them that you have contacted me?"

"We understand that pressure. But the community is not at risk from us. The community is at risk from whoever has our missing bomb. That has to be the priority now."

"The police might well feel that the priority is to let them deal with that risk."

"No. That's out."

"But you see my dilemma."

"Yes."

"What chance do I have of finding your bomb kit?"

"People's lives are at stake, Mr. Samson. We decided to make one attempt to forestall the possible consequences of our mistake. You are it. If you won't try to find the missing material, we'll all just read about it in the papers."

I didn't say anything.

The Frog said, "I do also need to make clear that there will be unpleasant consequences if you agree to honor our security and then break that trust."

"You're threatening me now?" And sounding a lot more like "real" terrorists.

"We have each gambled a great deal in the way of 'conventional' lives to work for the greater good. We will protect ourselves. Your mother lives here with her lover. We also know you have a girlfriend. We know where she lives and that she has a son and daughter. All I am saying is that you should not doubt the strength of our resolve."

"I think," I said, "that this interview is finished."

"Mr. Samson, if we find we can trust you, you'll find you can trust us. We have no wish to get you into difficulties about your license or . . . whatever. We just want the bomb found and made harmless. Please think seriously about the implications if you don't take the job on."

"I will think seriously about it," I said.

"If you are willing to go ahead, then call . . ." From inside her pocket she pulled a piece of paper with stuck-on digits cut from newspaper. "The number is for Channel 43 at Cab-Co. Use a public telephone. Say to whoever answers,

'Nature green in tooth and claw.' Then hang up. The police have the number tapped. Phone traces are done by computer now so they could have a patrol car wherever you call from within a couple of minutes. If you haven't made the call by midnight tonight then we'll all know what your priorities are."

I flattened the paper with the telephone number on the desk. I felt the weight of the situation. "Yes, O.K.," I said.

The Frog stood up. Almost instantly the three people on my bench stood up. They all went to the door and left.

"Have a nice day," I said as the door closed behind them.

I listened hard but I could barely hear as the Scum Front went down my stairs.

I GOT A DUSTPAN AND A brush. I swept up the pieces of broken cup.

Among the shards were six big bits. One at a time I shot them at my wastebasket. I *knew* they were all going to go in. I was that keyed up.

Every one a swish.

What kind of life is this? A simple man, in middle age, finally decides to surrender a piece of himself. He tries to be more like other people. He tries to care about making some bucks. And what happens? He gets bombers on his doorstep.

But are they nice average kill-everything-that-moves bombers? No, no. That would be too easy. They are "socially responsible" bombers. They are bombers who don't like to blow things up.

I stood.

I emptied the pan.

I needed to bang my head with a hammer. To jump out a second-floor window. To get mugged. *Anything* to command my attention for a while. To clear my head.

It was all very well for bombers to moralize about people being at risk. But was it *my* job to get involved? My *job*?

I remembered the Frog's hands. Not the hands of a young woman. Hands with a tan.

I wished I'd looked more closely at the Animals' clothes. Sneakers, yes, but Reeboks or Keds?

Who the hell were these people?

Three grown-ups and a kid: "Please, mister, help me find my bomb."

Shouldn't I just call the police now? Let the cops find the missing "item."

That was what I should do, wasn't it?

Where does one learn how to make a bomb? Did it mean one of them had been in the army?

But you still have to get the explosive materials.

They did use dynamite, and with its use on farms and in quarries maybe getting it was not that much of a problem. But explosive contacts *and* tanned hands?

Rings on the fingers?

And bells up my nose.

Shut up, jerk.

I went to my refrigerator for a carton of orange juice. I put a lot of ice cubes in a glass.

Then I put the orange juice back and just chewed the ice. Cold. Shock. Clarity.

I had no idea what these people looked like in civilian clothes. I could pass one on the street and not have a clue.

That was the point of the masks and long jackets, of course. And the high-pitched voice. The Bear and the Gorilla hadn't said anything at all, the perfect disguise.

Hey, I had them on tape.

I went back to my office and opened the drawer with the recorder inside. It seemed to be working all right. I stopped it, rewound the tape and pushed Play. "Oh, terrific," I heard myself say. "A breakout from the zoo?"

My telephone rang. Real life. Not a recording.

I stopped the tape.

I did nothing for several seconds.

But the whining, persistent, intrusive, ugly bell was too much for me. I finally gave in and answered.

My caller was Jerry Miller.

Captain Miller.

Of the police.

MY HEART BEAT WILDLY. I struggled for breath. I said, "How you doing, Jer?" and hoped he couldn't read my mind.

But he was listening to his own drum machine. "I'm doing great," he said. "Janie just left to visit an aunt in Noblesville and I'm about to step out."

"Ah," I said. Miller has had a . . . "friend" for quite a while now. Wendy's in local television. Miller's a lot happier than he used to be. Since his promotion.

He said, "So, when does your big TV advertising campaign start?"

"What?"

"I thought you were having a commercial made."

"Oh. Yeah. Yeah."

"Is there going to be a press launch? Beauty queens draped over your magnifying glass?"

I managed to say, "I've got this guy. He's making the ad. He's working on the footage now."

"Good," Miller said. "Great. But I'll need to know when it's scheduled. I've got some eye trouble that makes me blink a lot."

In a good mood, Miller.

Then he said, "Wondered if you wanted to come down for lunch tomorrow."

My heart sprinted again. "Let me check."

I put my hand over the phone and closed my eyes.

"Well?" I heard him say.

"Yeah," I said, unable to invent the simplest lie. "Let's do some lunch. I'll call you in the morning."

"Good," he said. "Al, there's some wild stuff going on. You'll be interested."

"Oh yeah?"

"Our Scummy friends called in their weekly bomb but when the guys got there, nothing."

"Oh yeah?"

"I figure they never planted it and they're seeing if they can get the publicity anyway."

"Yeah?"

He cleared his throat. "What we got here is minimalist bombers."

He waited for me to comment. When I didn't he said, "That's bombers who don't blow things up becoming bombers who don't even leave bombs."

He wanted me to say, "You never used to use words like 'minimalist.'" I said it.

"Yeah," he said happily. "Well, I read now."

A policeman in love.

He said, "At least that conniving bastard at the cable company didn't play this time. It's bad enough he gets in bed with them at all, but if he'd given them airtime when they hadn't actually laid anything down, well, that would have been real bad."

"Yeah," I said. "Look, Jer, I've got to go."

"Me too. Be lucky."

We hung up.

And I sat.

And I wondered if, by saying nothing to him, I had made whatever decision there was to make.

I WENT OUT.

I drove slowly, in no particular direction at first. Then I went to a part of the near south side that I know well and I did the alleys and the one-ways till even my paranoid self was pretty sure no one was following me.

Unless they had tagged my car electronically.

But they wouldn't have electronic tags.

Would they?

I popped out onto Kentucky Avenue and went southwest till I found a shopping mall. In it was a steak house.

I could nurse a meal for a while.

I parked in a cluster of cars. But when I walked toward the restaurant I saw a public phone on the wall between a drugstore and a chiropractic clinic and I realized I wanted the telephone more than any damn food.

I fumbled for quarters and called my woman.

She was not at home. Then I remembered she wasn't going to be there but I couldn't remember why.

I went into the steak house, took a tray and ordered a coffee.

"Coffee? That's all?" a fat cracker in red and white stripes asked me.

I said, "Uh, no. Give me a baked potato and a tossed salad."

"Hey, fella, y'know you're in the wrong place if you're a fuckin' vegetarian."

I stood back. I looked at him as he looked at me with insouciant pleasure from having so easily identified someone "different."

"Somethin' up your nose, fella?"

"You're right," I said. "I think maybe I am in the wrong place."

I left.

I followed the mall sidewalk back to the drugstore and I tracked around the aisles for a while.

When I got to the Indy 500 decorations I stopped.

Suddenly I wanted to talk to my kid.

But I knew what she would say. She would have me up to my neck in Bomber Animals and masks and funny voices and she would laugh all the way. An action-junkie, my kid. A quiet evening at home was practice for the grave as far as she was concerned.

I smiled. I laughed for a moment.

My little girl, little absent girl.

A woman nearby in a sepia satin jacket didn't know I was smiling for the kid.

She thought I was working up to making a pass. So she said, "Dream off, sucker."

"What?"

"No way, old-timer," she said. She picked up a 500 Party Pack and six checkered flags and walked away.

It seemed appropriate to move in the opposite direction.

I found myself channeled toward the checkout. I picked up a chocolate bar. I paid cash.

Outside I walked back to the telephone. I called the number at Cab-Co. I said, "Nature green in tooth and claw." I hung up.

I looked around, suddenly aware that my phone conversation would sound one shrimp short of a cocktail if anyone was listening. I was afraid that sepia-satin-jacket-woman was stalking me with a white net.

But I was alone.

I stood for several seconds while my heart slowed and then I walked back to my car and got in.

Looking for my keys I found the chocolate bar. I unwrapped it without tearing the paper and then took a little bite.

I turned the radio on for company. A D.J. tried to sell me chain pizza, so I turned the sound down till I couldn't distinguish the words.

I let the chocolate dissolve.

Some music began. I turned the sound up and hummed along.

I bit again.

I had half the bar left when the cops came.

The first car squealed in. It was followed by two others as quickly as flies follow shit.

My windshield was a TV set. I watched the patrolmen congregate by the phone. One of them opened a package and took from it the tape they use to mark a restricted area.

A fourth car pulled up and didn't bother to park neatly, so I had to go the long way around to the mall exit when I decided to change channels.

The first cop had arrived four and a half minutes after I made the call.

20

MOM WAS IN HER BATHROBE, alone with the television, when I knocked on her living room door. "Come in, son," she said. She turned the sound down.

"Did you have a good Sunday outing?" I asked.

She looked at me. "Is something wrong, Albert? Does it have something to do with that strange girl you brought down here?"

I intended to say "No." But I hesitated.

"She's too young for you, son."

I was picking an amused denial when Norman pushed through behind me.

We looked at each other.

He said, "Oh." He turned around and went out again.

Mom said, "She might seem exciting at first but you've lived through whole decades she's never heard of, so you'll run out of things to talk about."

I said, "It's not like that."

"You don't mind some motherly advice, though, do you, son?"

"Of course not."

"Don't let your imagination get the better of you. That's all I've got to say." With that she returned to the TV.

I left and closed the door behind me.

But as I walked toward the foot of the stairs that led to my rooms Norman materialized from some dark fissure. "Well?" he asked.

"Well what?"

"For Christ's sake!" he said. He stomped past me toward the living room.

Back in my office I found I hadn't turned on my answering machine when I went out.

That irritated me beyond its importance. It was an error of routine, the rules that the new me had set for the new life.

Not a big deal, but . . . Either I played this game or I didn't.

After a few moments of self-flagellation I forgave myself. And as a reward my brain remembered why my woman was not available to still my anguished outpourings: she was at a meeting of a foster parents' support group.

I decided to read. I went to my bedroom and picked *Chance & Necessity* from the shelves that line the wall next to the bed. It's about the origins of life. Well, my life was at a new beginning. Maybe I could pick up some tips.

And then I heard a knock.

But it was not the Scum Front on the porch outside the office. It was Mom at the door that connects me to the rest of her house.

She said, "I meant to say, son, if you're in some kind of trouble, I have a gun now."

"You what?"

"You can borrow it if you need it."

"A gun? What do you mean, a gun?"

She drew a small-caliber automatic pistol from her bathrobe pocket and showed it to me.

"Is that thing loaded?"

"There's not much point if it isn't. But the safety catch is on. See?"

I saw. "Whatever possessed you to get one of those things?"

"It's not the tool," she said, "it's how the tool is used."

"Which doesn't answer the question."

"Oh, it just seemed like a good idea," she said. "I think a widow is entitled to a little protection."

"Is this one of Norman's suggestions?"

"Don't mind Norman, son. He means well."

"Does he?"

"Oh yes," she said. "Though he's a little rough, I admit."

"You're not about to tell me he's a diamond underneath, I hope."

"He certainly is a help."

"Do you know that he disapproves of my living and working here? That he thinks I am taking advantage of you?"

"Oh yes. But I told him that you'll pay me rent once you get solid on your feet."

"That won't be long now, Mom," I said. I meant it to sound strong but it sounded feeble.

"I'm sure it won't," she said.

"I'm having some television ads made. They'll be hitting the airwaves soon."

"Oh, good. Which channel?"

"One of the ones on the new cable system."

"Oh."

"I'm going to sign you up for that, if you don't mind. I'll pay for it, of course."

"Well, we'll see," she said. Then, "Would you like the gun, son?"

"Don't point that thing at me, please!"

"I'm not going to shoot you. I've been practicing."

"Where?"

"There's a range in one of the shopping centers out Southeastern. I've been the last two Sundays."

"With Norman?"

"It's a lot of fun. And I'm getting better. I hit the target most every time now."

"You'll be wanting a bigger gun for your birthday, with a

grip made to measure and a stabilizer to reduce the lift from the recoil."

"Oh no," she said. "Not yet. But remember, son, it's here if you need it."

"I'll remember, Mom."

"That's good."

"O.K."

She looked up at me. "Albert, are things all right?"

"Sure."

"It's funny, you know. A boy like you suddenly going about your business so differently after all these years. I hope you're not trying to be something you aren't. We aren't all meant to be successful, son, but we are all meant to be ourselves."

"Everything's fine."

"Then you bring down a strange young woman . . .   I don't know. I just don't know."

"There's nothing to worry about, Mom."

"I wish I could believe that," she said, as if talking to herself. Then, "Would you like to come down and play Scrabble with Norman and me?"

"I think I'll pass this time. Thanks for asking."

"You probably have some work to do, now you're so busy."

"That's right. I'm expecting a call."

Even as I said it, the telephone rang.

21

MY CALLER, HOWEVER, was Quentin Quayle. "Albert, it's going wrong!"

"Sorry to hear that."

"I may have to end it all!"

"It can't be a suicide matter, surely."

In a voice that was calm and corrective, he said, "Don't be stupid. That's not what I meant."

"Oh."

"But I need to talk to you immediately."

"You do?"

"Come now. Take whatever is necessary out of the money I gave you, but come."

"Don't you think you're being a little bit—"

"Please!" he said.

A magic word, especially in conjunction with the fact that waiting for the Scummies was making me jumpy. I said, "O.K."

Poet had the use of a third-floor apartment on a corner of 38th Street and North Meridian. It took me the best part of twenty minutes to get to his door and when he opened it, he said, "Oh, Albert!" with an over-the-top emotional exhalation that, on screen, would have made movies silent again.

I didn't get an immediate chance to ask him what his problem was. He turned and walked away from me. As he did so he pulled at his hair with a baby's anger.

I wasn't so sure that responding to my soulmate's summons had been a good idea after all, but I entered the apartment and closed the door.

The living room was chock-a-block with furniture and ornaments. Quayle couldn't have packed it that way in mere months so perhaps this was an apartment that Charlotte Vivien kept specially for poets.

I'd never been in the building before but it was where a local politician conducted a personal affirmative action program. According to Miller.

Quayle draped himself across a flowery settee behind a glass-topped coffee table with bronze legs.

I used a straight-backed chair and sat opposite him.

"I'm destroyed. We were going to have such a lovely life! Charlotte has another man."

"Is that what this is about?"

"Of course."

"Who is it?"

"Oh I have no idea."

"Well, how do you know?"

"Charlotte is suddenly less open with me."

I waited. There wasn't any more. "That's it?"

"Yes."

"Poet, didn't you say she had her children home this weekend and that she was upset?"

"She is *less open*. I have been a confidant and suddenly I'm not. She's got a man, Albert. Sure as eggs is eggs, Charlotte Vivien is seeing somebody. I am *never* wrong about this kind of thing."

"If you say so."

"I say so."

I said, "That's the ball game. Time to be a good sport, wish her luck and forget her."

He sat up and leaned forward. He looked at the floor, and the hanging hair meant I couldn't see his face at all. "But I don't want to forget her," he said.

"What choice have you got?"

He threw his head back and said, "I want you to follow her."

"What?"

"I can't revise my strategy until I know who the opposition is."

"Poet, following Charlotte Vivien is not what you hired me to do."

"I hired your professional services. Isn't following unfaithful women the very essence of what private detectives do?"

"It takes a lot of time. I have other jobs."

"Just follow her at night. That will do. Evenings. I'm sure she is not the sort of woman who would do it in daylight."

I looked at him. "I suppose you're never wrong about that kind of thing either."

"You *must* do it," he said pathetically.

"Well, I can hire other people to follow her when I'm too busy."

"Whatever it takes."

"But your money won't last long."

"I'll give you more."

"Poet, are you sure about this?"

"Yes."

"Aren't you panicking? Don't you want to give it some time to feel better?"

"No."

I said nothing.

He said, "Albert, haven't you ever been in love?"

I considered things as I went down the stairs. A simple tail on Charlotte Vivien wouldn't be hard to arrange. Graham Parkis had "guys and gals" just waiting for the work. And I had a home number for him.

Well, all right.

There was a telephone booth across 38th Street and I went to it.

However, the number I called was Charlotte Vivien's.

I expected Loring to answer but the voice was a girl's. "Hello?"

"May I speak to Mrs. Vivien?"

"Who's calling, please?"

No matter what Mom said, it was not a time to be by myself.

"This is the Chief of Police."

"Oh, hi, Chief."

"Uh, hi."

"This is Sheree. Mom's not here now, but can I take a message?"

"No thanks, Sheree," I said. "No message."

"Hey, I watched you this afternoon."

"You did?"

"On the VCR. The tape of Mom's party."

"Oh, yeah. I haven't had a chance to see it yet. Too much work."

"You were great."

"Good. Good."

"And I thought that detective Mom hired was mega-fabulous. When he sneezed on that powder and it went in his face! Wow, that was *so* funny! He was just darling."

"You think so?"

"I'd *really* like to meet him. Do you know him?"

"Slightly."

"Is he an actor or something?"

"I do understand that he's got a little television coming up," I said.

WITH CHARLOTTE VIVIEN not at home I was relieved of any imperative to organize surveillance of her. Can't tell a guy or a gal to follow someone if you don't know where the someone is. Right? Am I right?

I headed home. I was hungry.

I wasn't back long enough to get a mouthful when the bell rang.

I knew who it was going to be. I went to the desk and turned on the tape recorder. Then I answered the door.

It was the Bear and the Frog. No Kate King or Gorilla.

"Where the *hell* have you been?" the Frog asked me in her high "funny" voice. "What do you think this is? A game?"

"What do you expect? The rest of my life to stop? I made your call to Channel 43 but then I had another client to visit."

"You also used a telephone," the Bear said. She too spoke at an artificial pitch, but low-voiced. Almost a growl. "At 38th and Meridian."

"That's perfectly true," I said.

"Was it to the police?" Bear asked.

"No," I said. "Not this time."

The Frog fumed behind her mask. "Don't you *care* that somebody might die while you mess around?"

"If what you want is buttons to push, go find a soft-drink machine. You coming in or not?"

They came in.

"Sit down," I said. "Once you're comfortable I'll tell you my conditions for taking this job."

"*Your* conditions?" the Bear said.

"Your hearing is acute." I brought a second chair from the bedroom and I faced them across the desk.

"What we're talking here is a job, not club membership. So I'll need money for my time and my expenses. A couple of thousand dollars to start. I will account for it in detail but not on paper. Do you have that much with you?"

"Yes," she said.

"I'll need a way to contact you if I have to."

The Bear said, "What, you mean like a phone number?"

"That would be ideal."

"No. Absolutely not."

"Well, think up something else. But I need a way to get in touch in a hurry."

The Animals looked at each other.

"We'll see what we can do," the soprano Frog said.

"I won't go to the police about you, but if they come to me, what I do will depend on the pressure they apply."

"We thought it might," the Frog said.

"Finally," I said, "while the job lasts you will plant *no more bombs.*"

They exchanged looks but said nothing.

"I have a license to protect. If the police find out I'm working for you I will need a compelling reason why I didn't come to them at the beginning. The fact that I was able to keep you from planting more bombs is that reason. Do you understand and agree to my conditions?"

The Frog looked at the Bear, who nodded. The Frog said, "Yes."

"I was afraid you would," I said.

23

IT WAS THE FROG WHO LEFT the missing bomb. "I got
to the Merchants Bank Building about three-thirty."

"The lobby?"

"No. There's a parking lot next to it and a connecting
walkway. You come in on the fifth floor."

"You had the bomb with you?"

"In an Ayres plastic shopping bag."

"I take it you weren't wearing your mask."

"A lightweight houndstooth wool coat and a black velvet
hat."

"Not clothes you ordinarily wear?"

"Correct," she said. "And I also wore a blond wig and
glasses."

"What did you do next?"

"I took an elevator to the fourth."

"What's there?"

"It's part of a law office. I got out and looked around until
the elevator left. Then I acted like I was on the wrong floor.
I asked the receptionist where the stairs were. She pointed
down the hall and I went to them."

"I see."

"One floor down is a women's rest room. Well, on the door it says 'omen.' I went in and took my hat off and put on sunglasses."

"Oh yes?"

"The kind of society this is," the Bear interjected, "anybody passing her on the stairs would only remember 'blond' and 'sunglasses.'" The Bear emphasized her words with hand gestures. Her hands were narrow, with long fingers which looked no younger—though less tanned—than the Frog's.

I waited.

The Frog said, "Then, in the stairwell, I went up and looked for a place to leave my package."

"Did anybody see you?"

"No. No one used the stairs."

"And?"

"I went to the fire hose closet on the sixth."

"The what?"

"Every landing in the stairwell has a closet marked 'Fire Hose.' They're all left unlocked, and inside, the loops of hose hang down to the floor. It's a perfect place to leave a bomb."

"Where, exactly?"

"I taped it to the back wall. Then I closed the door again."

"And it wasn't noticeable?"

"Absolutely not, unless you were looking for it."

"And then?"

"I left the stairs at the fifth floor and went back to my car."

"And you didn't see anybody on the stairs?"

"No."

"What about in the corridor, or in the parking lot?"

The Frog considered. "A woman got in the elevator with me when I came in, but she punched the first-floor button. And I did see two people on the fifth floor on my way out. But they were laughing and didn't notice me. I think they were headed for the snack bar."

"What time did you leave the building?"

"I was out before four."

"In your wig?"

"I took it off in the car."

"And you went where?"

"About my own business," she said pointedly.

"Well," I said, "it doesn't sound like anybody picked your bomb up by pure accident."

"We agree," the Bear growled.

"But maybe someone you didn't notice saw you behaving strangely."

The Frog didn't think so, but she said, "It's conceivable."

"Or maybe somebody followed you all the way."

I expected an immediate and clear rejection of this idea because nobody was supposed to know who they were. Instead there was a hesitation and the two Animals glanced at each other.

"Look, you've got something to say. Let's get to it, all right?"

"There was this man," the Frog said.

I waited.

"When we bought our explosives there was a little hitch."

"A 'little hitch'?"

"We arranged to buy some dynamite, caps, timers, right? But when we made the pickup we saw a man who seemed to take an interest in us."

"Where was this?"

The Bear glanced at the Frog and said, "Well, you know the rubble belt . . ."

"The what?"

"All the empty houses north of downtown that have been boarded up and left to rot. Perfectly good houses—in fact some beautiful houses."

"Yes, I know them," I said.

Just beyond the current "gentrification" there is a corridor of decay. The "rubble belt": not a bad name for it.

"Well," the Bear said, "we met our supplier just north of 23rd Street behind an empty house."

"How many of you were there?"

"All four."

"How did you carry what you bought?"

"In suitcases," the Frog said. "But it's not as if we walked the streets. We parked in front of the house and went to what used to be a garage in the backyard. Our supplier was waiting in his car. We paid him and he got the suitcases out of his trunk."

"But then," the Bear said. "I noticed this man walking toward us. He was maybe a couple of hundred feet away."

"What did you do?"

"I pointed him out to our supplier."

"And he said?"

"Not to worry about him. To be precise, he said, 'Don't worry 'bout no wino, hon.'"

"But you didn't think he was a wino?"

"He had a paper bag, but I didn't see him do anything with it. I *felt* that he was interested," the Bear said. "He seemed attentive."

"Could he have been a policeman?"

"That's what we were afraid of. But he didn't seem like a policeman either."

"So what happened?"

The Bear said, "When we carried the bags back to our car, I didn't get in. I circled round the house to see if the guy stayed put or followed us or what."

"And?"

"He moved to where he could see us on the street."

"Well, well," I said. "What did he look like?"

"Black. Or rather, African-American. Quite tall, over six feet. Very thin. Dark. Short hair with a razor-cut part. He was maybe thirty. And his clothes were not very good."

"Did he see you?"

"No."

"And then?"

"He walked to the garage and looked around. Then he walked down the alley to 24th Street. There was an old flat-back there."

"Flat-back?"

"Pickup truck. That's what we called them when I was a kid. Where I grew up."

I didn't ask where that was.

The Bear said, "I got the license plate number." She had a slip of paper ready. Like the telephone number they'd given me before, it was a paste-up job.

I said, "The guy showed interest at a critical time. Do you have any other reason to believe he's involved?"

The Frog said, "I think I saw the man again later."

"Where was that?"

"No," she said. She shook her head. "I'm not going to tell you."

"Near where you live?"

"Yes."

"What was he doing when you saw him?"

"He stood in the street and looked at the house. He stayed there for quite a long time."

I asked, "How would he know where you lived?"

"I think," she said, "because the car we moved the explosives in was mine. We thought there was no risk. It was a lesson. I got rid of it right away."

If he had located her from her license plate it would raise questions about who the guy might be and who he might know.

The Frog said, "I *could* be wrong about it being him."

"But you don't think so."

"No."

"How long ago did you buy the dynamite?"

"The beginning of February," the Frog said.

"And when did you see the man again?"

"About a week later."

"So nothing has happened for nearly three months?"

"Not until now."

Not exactly a hot lead. I said, "How did you find a cooperative dynamite salesman?"

"The original contact was not made here," the Bear said.

"So the man you dealt with wasn't local?"

"Oh, he was local," the Bear said. "But I made the initial contact in Boston."

I frowned. "What are we talking about? An Irish connection?"

"Our plan," the Bear said, "was to use a plastic explosive called semtex. That turned out to be hard to get, but in Boston I found someone who gave me the name of a man who would sell us dynamite here. But he's not involved, I'm sure."

The Frog nodded, so I said, "Is there anything else at all that might help me?"

They looked at each other. "No," the Frog said.

"O.K.," I said. "But I want to tell you something."

"What?" the Frog said.

"Tomorrow I am having lunch with a friend of mine in the police. I don't know if you are going to waste more time and energy following me around but I just thought I'd tell you now so you don't get the wrong idea."

Ah, but what constitutes the rightness or wrongness of an idea? As soon as I closed the door behind them I got the idea to call my woman.

She was home but she said, "I didn't expect to hear from you tonight. Is there some problem?"

"I've just been talking to the Scum Front," I said. "But don't tell anybody."

"Al, I've had a hard meeting and I'm not feeling very well and I'm in the middle of a conversation with Lucy. I'm not really in the mood for jokes."

I said, "No, I can see that. Sorry, kid. Poor taste." Shortly afterward we hung up.

24

HOW SIMPLE IS LIFE MEANT to be?

In the morning I went to the Merchants Bank Building. I took the elevator to the fourth floor. I got off. I faced a young woman who sat behind a crescent-shaped desk.

And as soon as I approached she looked up and said, "May I help you?"

I said, "I hope so."

And she said, "I hope so too."

Life isn't like that. There had to be a catch.

"May I ask," I said, "were you here Friday afternoon?"

"Oh, it's about the bomb scare."

I smiled. "Are you the Scum Front? Do I claim my reward?"

"They didn't leave one, and if they did it wouldn't have gone off," she said, "but it's awful scary, isn't it? I mean, the idea of a bomb, here. It's . . . like an intrusion."

"It is indeed," I said. "But I'm not interested in bombs."

"Oh good," she said. "I was so upset I couldn't keep my mind on my dancing all weekend."

"You danced all weekend?"

"It's my other job."

"Ah," I said.

"What do you want?"

"It's about a woman. She got off the elevator here a little after three-thirty on Friday."

"Oh, you mean the woman in the houndstooth coat?"

"You remember her?"

"She must be real popular," the dancing girl said.

My heart beat faster because I knew what she was going to say next. I delivered my cue: "Why do you say that?"

"Because somebody else asked me about her."

"When?"

"Friday afternoon."

"What time? Do you remember?"

"Oh, just a couple of minutes after she got off."

"The somebody else . . . ?"

"It was this Negro woman in a *very* expensive café au lait dress with tiny covered buttons down the front."

"And what did she want to know about the woman in the houndstooth coat?"

"If I'd seen her and where she went."

"And what did you say?"

"That she went to the stairs."

"And did the second woman go to the stairs too?"

"Yup."

"Did she say why she was asking?"

"No. She just asked," Dancing Girl said. "Like you."

We looked at each other.

I said, "I'm just a guy trying to do a job, miss, and if you can describe the second woman who came through around three-thirty Friday, that job would be made easier."

"Oh well," Dancing Girl said. "Let me think now. The skirt was cut on the bias and draped sarong style. It was a real light jersey knit. She wore black suede boots and she had these gold earrings, three loops one inside the other. And she was wearing funny gloves."

"Funny?"

"They were wool. They didn't go at all."

"Oh."

"She was maybe five six. Not fat or thin. And she wasn't one of the blue-black Negroes but she was pretty dark."

"Would you recognize her again?"

"Her? The person?"

"That's right."

"I don't know about that," she said. "I know I'm not supposed to say it these days, but they look kind of the same to me, those people."

All the affirmative action in the world wasn't going to make Dancing Girl more interested in human beings than in the clothes they wore.

"I'm going to level with you," I said.

"Oh yeah?"

"I'm a private detective." I took my license out and held it up for her to study.

"Gee," she said, "you know, I *thought* you were weird."

"That woman in the café au lait dress is someone I need to find. I think you could help a lot if you would let me come back with an artist."

"An artist?"

"Someone to try to draw her from what you tell him."

"Oh, I don't know."

"We could do it here. Or we could do it after work. Whatever would be convenient for you."

"I don't want to get mixed up in anything."

"There won't be any trouble. It's not like that."

"I still don't know."

"I can pay you for your time, if that would help."

It helped.

I used her telephone to call Graham Parkis.

"Yeah," he said. "I got a little gal who does stuff like that. She's terrific. She ought to be able to get downtown by, oh, two-thirty, three."

But Dancing Girl preferred to do it after work, so we arranged a meeting in the building lobby shortly after five.

"It's going to cost you, Samson," Parkis said to me.

"How much?"

He said a number. I agreed without dickering.

I left Dancing Girl and walked up the stairs to the sixth-floor landing.

I found the fire hose closet and opened the door.

It was exactly as described, filled with looped cloth hose.

A bomb taped to the back wall would only be found by somebody looking for it.

MILLER, IN THE MIDDLE of a Monday, looked far less jaunty than he'd sounded on the phone the day before.

"Don't even ask," he said as I sat across from him.

But I'd had a good morning. "I wouldn't believe what's been going on inside IPD, right?"

"Damn right you wouldn't."

I laughed for a moment, but he seemed to think I was about as amusing as an ayatollah.

I said, "You got to think about the good things in life, Jer. You got to remember there can't be flowers without rain."

"What's the deal here? You going to order, or what?"

We ordered.

But I persisted. "Cheer up," I said. "I've got a favor to ask, just like the old days."

He narrowed his eyes and tried to see inside my brain. That was like the old days too. It constituted an advance of mood.

"It's a license plate number. I want to know the name and address of the owner."

"Oh yeah? What's that about?"

"It's a hot lead to finding the Scum Front."

"Oh," he said.

I wrote the number on a napkin.

"Yeah, all right. If I get a chance," he said. He put the napkin in his pocket.

I said, "One day you're practically humping the phone with jokes and the next day I can't hardly get no civil word outta ya. Is something up? Janie come home early? Did the fair Wendy tell you about her other boyfriend, or her girl-friend?"

"No, no. Nothing like that."

"Well, what is it like?"

He stirred the sugar bowl. "I went into work today."

"That'll do it every time."

"See, the politicians are fuckin'-A bitched off because we haven't caught the Scummies yet. We were all pulling to-gether there for a while, but now guys that patched up arguments are back fighting for territory. The whole thing's shit."

"So what *is* happening with the Scum Front?"

He looked at me. "Happening? Nothing's happening, that's what's happening."

"So there wasn't a bomb?"

"They called one in. Merchants Bank Building. Did I tell you?"

"Yeah. But you said when your guys went to collect it no one was home."

"Right."

"So there really wasn't one?" I asked. "It's not that they found it but decided to say they hadn't? To cut off the publicity?"

"That was considered a few weeks ago," he said.

"Was it?"

"Nobody wanted to take the responsibility, in case it made the Scummies angry and pushed them into blowing someplace up."

"I can see that," I said.

"But the same nobodies are happy to put thumbscrews on everybody else. And when pressure is applied to people

who are already busting their guts to catch the bad guys, all
that happens is they begin to think about protecting their
butts."

That too I could see.

"So by screaming blue murder the politicians make it
less likely they're going to get what they want."

Our food came.

Miller and I have had more entertaining conversations. I
might have done his mood some good by changing the
subject to childhood or Vice President jokes. But I had my
own problems. I asked him whether IPD had any serious
leads on the Scum Front.

"Leads?" He laughed, but it wasn't for fun. "They got
nothing and they spend all day looking at it. They go through
every place they know the Scummies have been and pick up
every scrap of paper and piece of fingerprint and bit of dust
and they fill the labs with it. They got a whole computer full
of *information*. But they got no *knowledge* whatsoever."

"You sound like a fortune cookie."

"Yeah," he said. A little smile. "You know what I think?"
he said. "You want to know what I think?"

"What do you think?"

"I think we're not going to catch them till they do
goddamned blow something up. That's what I think."

"Oh."

"I just hope it's themselves. Or the goddamned people
protecting them."

"Protecting them?"

"Come on, Al! Somebody knows who they are. Got to.
But in the last four weeks we haven't had a tenth the phone
calls we had at the beginning. That's because the bombs don't
go off. The public likes them now. It's crazy, because they're
fucking dangerous. But people aren't worried the way they
used to be. And if they don't make a mistake, it's going to take
somebody getting killed."

I nodded with sympathy.

"Meanwhile the Department goes from bad to worse.

Used to be *merely* the troops not getting support from the top. Now the whole thing's coming to pieces."

I waited for him; he had more to say.

"Hey, you know what the psycho guys say?"

"What psycho guys? I thought all you guys were psycho."

"The Criminal Psychological Profile Consultants, Albert. You don't think in a major investigation we're not going to take advantage of the brainy gentlemen who think they can close their eyes and mental up a picture of our perpetrators. Just pass them a sketch pad and a set of fucking crayons."

"What do they say?"

"You'll like this," he said.

"Promise?"

"They say the Scum Front is made up of people who aren't normal."

I laughed for him.

"Not normal. Good stuff, huh? See, they don't fit the 'typical terrorist profile.'"

"Oh."

"Most terrorists set off bombs, see. These don't."

"Got it."

"They think we're dealing with 'disaffected middle-class sociopaths.' Maybe guys who lost their jobs at one of the big companies, and maybe went nuts being at home with their wives."

"Oh."

"Ever since we got this high-powered analysis there have been guys doing nothing but working through lists of people that lost their jobs in this city the last couple of years. Think about the phone calls: 'Hello. You lose your job last year? Still out of work? Too bad. You haven't been leaving bombs around by any chance?'"

I smiled.

"You want to know how much the psycho-ologists charge to come up with crap like that?"

"Yeah. What?"

"I wish I knew. I'd go to fuckin' night school. I really would."

26

CAPTAIN MILLER WENT back to work. I stayed behind. The waiter asked if I wanted anything else. I ordered another napkin.

"Was that to use here or shall I wrap it to go?" he said, talking himself out of a tip. But he probably thought it was worth it.

I needed the napkin to doodle on while I thought about the woman in wool gloves that didn't go with her café au lait dress. She was the hot favorite as the person who picked up the bomb. Discovering her existence was a major piece of luck.

But there was no time for celebration. Delay might result in just the explosion and death Miller was so confident of. I felt the pressure; I needed to find Wool Glove Woman.

Of course the artist's drawing was the next big step, but I would need to show it to someone. Here the Animal brigade was clearly my best bet. If Wool Glove Woman knew to follow the Frog, the Frog might well know who Wool Glove Woman was.

The problem was that I did not yet have a way to get in touch with the Animals.

So I packed my napkin and went home. Maybe the Scummies had acceded to my requirement. Maybe I was still on a roll.

I had a visitor when I returned to my office, all right. But it did not hop, growl or beat its chest.

Quentin Quayle looked awful. Sleeplessness did not agree with him. Nor, perhaps, did sitting on my office stairs through May showers.

He stood up as I opened the door.

I unlocked the office and went in.

He didn't need an embossed invitation.

"I'm so cold," he said. "Where have you been?"

"Working, Poet. I told you I'm busy."

I went to my desk. There had been seven calls but I didn't want to play the messages in public. I found an earplug and said, "Excuse me a minute," while he sorted himself out on the chair.

Five of the calls were from him. But another was from Frank, who said that he'd pulled a few strings and that the first of my TV ads would be broadcast on Cab-Co tonight. The seventh call was without a message.

By the time I began the rewinding procedure, Quentin Quayle was comfortable enough to be irritated.

"I am paying you," he said.

When I didn't answer—it wasn't a question, was it?—he said, "Well?"

"You want your money back?"

"Have you achieved anything with this work you've been out doing all day?"

"Quite a lot," I said, "but I haven't looked for Charlotte Vivien's gentleman friend yet."

"Why not?"

"For one thing, your instruction was to follow her late afternoons and at night."

For another I had forgotten about her, but good Go-for-It Detectives don't share that kind of tiny truth with clients.

He said morosely, "She's been out all day and I don't know where."

"Are you saying you want her followed day and night?"

"No, no."

"Well, what have you been calling me about?"

"I thought it might help if you had a photograph of Charlotte."

"I have met the woman. Even worked for her. Bowed though my head was in her august presence, I would recognize her again."

"You don't have to be snotty," he said. "You don't have to kick a man just because he is down and in love."

He was right, of course. You don't have to. It can feel good, though.

But I said, "Sorry. If you have a photograph of her, I would be pleased to have it."

A hangdog looked up and said, "Would you?"

"Pathos makes me borborygmic, Poet. Just give me the picture."

He passed an envelope across the desk. It had a thin pink ribbon around it.

I found scissors. Inside was a pack of some twenty photographs.

I leafed through them. Charlotte Vivien in almost every conceivable daytime-around-the-house pose. Any one of ten would do for identification purposes.

But I became aware that this was an attractive woman.

I hadn't noticed during the tense days leading up to the party. Then she had just seemed obsessed with what a hysterically funny idea the party was.

In these pictures, however, her face was lively and expressive. She seemed comfortable with the photographic scrutiny and her eyes, especially, came alive as I thumbed through the shots. Quentin's preoccupation might not be with her bank balance after all.

I pulled one of the facial full frontals and said, "Thanks."

"You're welcome."

"Now, how about a few more details? She's about forty, right?"

"Forty-seven."

I looked at the picture again. "You said she has children."

"Two. Both at college. Usually."

"And she has a lot of interests and activities?"

"She's very active," he said.

"When you go home, I want you to write out a list of the organizations she belongs to with details of where their meetings are held and who might be there. O.K.?"

"I can do that," he said.

"And you don't know where she is now?"

"No."

"But she's coming back later this afternoon?"

"There are a dozen people from the Butler dance and drama department coming over for cocktails."

"So if someone is ready to follow her after that . . ."

"Great," Quayle said.

Then he started to cry.

That passed my chicken limit. "On your way, Poet. Go home and write the list. Make it rhyme."

He rose and began to gather his outdoor clothing. But he moved slowly and sniffed a lot.

I said, "I don't buy this feeble stuff, Poet. I think it's a Scarlet Pimpernel act while all the time you're the brains behind the Scum Front. Don't think I haven't noticed they only showed up after you hit town."

For a moment, his eyes lit up. "You've read Baroness Emmuska Orczy?"

"Just the Classic Comic."

That hit harder than any of the cracks I'd aimed directly at him.

"What *am* I doing here?" he said. "In this . . . this . . . desert."

And despite myself, I felt the loneliness and I was affected.

He looked at me with half a smile. "I wasn't always the Quentin Quayle you see before you."

"You weren't?"

"I am my own creation. I was born a 'George.' I became 'Quentin.' The alliteration seemed a good career move."

"Oh."

"I used to be in love with my life. Now I am in Indiana with my love."

He said the second "love" as if he wasn't having a real good time.

I said, "But you were always a Quayle?"

"Oh yes."

I went to the door. "If you want something to make you feel better, stop at the luncheonette downstairs. Ask for Mom and say I sent you. Order some of her chili. It's good for love."

When he left I called Graham Parkis again. I wanted him to supply someone to cover Charlotte Vivien for a few days.

"Well, well," Parkis said. "Things must be on the move down your end of the market."

"I have a photograph of the target and I know where she'll be from late this afternoon. Can your operative come downtown with your artist? That should give him or her plenty of time to get up to the house before the target goes out."

"You don't care whether it's a man or a woman?"

"Not in the slightest."

"In that case what about if the artist *is* the operative? We know she's available."

"She's used to surveillance?"

"Oh yes."

"Can she do the picture and still get to the north side before seven?"

"If you and your witness are punctual, there should be no problem at all."

"Sold," I said.

"I'll give her a call now. She'll be pleased to have the work. She's got a mother who's not well. It's run up some bills."

I hung up and chewed an antacid. I get awful indigestion when I'm force-fed on sob stories.

27

I CALLED MILLER. MAYBE the trace on the license plate number was back. But he wasn't at his desk. I was a little surprised. I thought being a captain meant you never had to go out. But what do I know?

Then I tried Frank, about my commercials.

He was out too.

It was a little after three. Until I went downtown at four-thirty all I could do was wait for the Scum Front to get in touch with me.

About three-thirty the telephone rang. I practically flew from sorting dirty clothes to answer it.

A woman's voice said, "Mr. Samson?"

"Yes."

"Bobbie Lee Leonard."

"Who?"

"I'm supposed to make a drawing for you, from a witness's description. And now I hear you want me to follow somebody."

"Ah, ah, ah."

"Is something wrong? Are you choking?"

"No no. I'm just expecting another call."

"You got call waiting or do you want me to free the line?"

"There's no need."

There was a hesitation.

"Really," I said.

"If you're sure," she said. "Well, reason I'm calling is I thought if we met up before seeing your witness, you could explain about the surveillance assignment. That way I could leave as soon as the drawing is done."

"Your suggestion sounds entirely, even spectacularly sensible," I said.

"Are you sure nothing's wrong, Mr. Samson?"

"No no. It's just that your clarity has gone to my head."

"You mind if I say you don't talk like anyone I ever worked for before?"

"Not at all, Ms Leonard."

"We're meeting your witness in the lobby of the Merchants Bank Building, right?"

"Right."

"I thought we could meet in the parking lot next to it. Say, at the top, four-thirty. Will that give you enough time to brief me?"

"That should be just fine. How will I know you?"

"Well, unless I get my carburetor back together quicker than I expect to, I'll be the one with dirty fingernails."

I laughed.

"Otherwise, chances are I will be the only woman with a sketch pad leaning on the hood of a red Rabbit."

When we hung up, the telephone rang again immediately.

It was Miller.

"I tried you a few minutes ago," I said, "but you weren't there."

"Anybody whose job entails a lot of sitting should make a habit of getting up for at least five minutes every hour."

"I can see those seminars they send you on aren't a total waste of taxpayers' money."

"You want details of this vehicle ownership, or not?"

* * *

The "flat-back" truck was nine years old and belonged to a Cecil Redman. Redman's address was on College Avenue between 22nd and 23rd Streets. It was not far from where the Scum Front had picked up its explosives.

I decided to use the time before my meeting with Bobbie Lee Leonard to look at Redman's house.

But when I got into my car I didn't start the engine.

On the passenger's seat was a manila envelope. I hadn't left it there when I came in. I hate a messy vehicle.

I opened the envelope and saw a newspaper cut-out message. It began, "To contact us put the white hanky in your office window."

I shook the envelope. A white handkerchief fell out.

The message continued, "When we see the hanky we will call your office and pick one of the locations listed below. Each has a public phone. Go to that phone. If you get no call within six minutes, go to the next phone. Six minutes the next and so on. From the bottom of the list, start again at the top." And there was a list of street corners numbered one through nine.

It ended, "Learn these locations and destroy this."

Cloak-and-dagger stuff all the way.

A handkerchief in my window?

I looked through the addresses of the telephones. They followed a geographical sequence and were short drives one to the next.

Well, I had my way to contact them, even if it was labor-intensive. It seemed they were prepared to spend hour after hour, day after day driving past my office.

But there wasn't time to try it out. My plan had been to look around near Cecil Redman's address. No reason to change it. I tucked the note and hanky back in the envelope and headed for College.

In fifteen minutes I was at the address Miller had given me. The building was a three-story clapboard-clad house that had once been white.

From the car I could see two faded aqua doors leading from a narrow, unrailed porch. Each bore a number and Redman's was next to a curtained sash window. The window beside the other door was larger but had no glass. It was only partly filled by a piece of hardboard.

Redman's pickup was not parked on the street.

I drove around the corner and then up the muddy alleyway that passed behind the building.

The truck was not here either but the back view of the house showed how much of it was empty and rotting. There was a gaping hole in the roof and another in the outside wall. None of the windows had glass.

However, Redman's building was not as ramshackle as the frame house beside it. Nor had it been originally so elegant. Next door there were the remains of a veranda around two full sides and gabled upper rooms looking out in all directions. I was particularly taken by an arch-shaped double door which had once led to a second-floor porch. Now, of course, it was nothing but a rotting hole.

The Bear's indignation about the "rubble belt" seemed suddenly appropriate. I hated the decay of the place. And I, a middle-aged man back living with his mother, identified with it. We were not far off the same age, the house and me, but it was prematurely old. Disease is one thing but to become infirm from neglect is hateful.

I'd have been thrilled to have the place. To have the chance to make it good again. It would make one hell of a base for a Go-for-It Detective to detect from.

I thought about all the little rooms and odd places I have worked from and lived in.

Funny how your stomach never suffers from your own sob stories.

My time was running out.

I drove on up the alley and completed the circuit that brought me back round to the front of Redman's.

I got out and went up to Redman's door. I listened for a moment but heard nothing from inside.

I went to the other door on the porch. Through the gap at the top of the window next to it I saw the sky.

As I turned away, a child came around a corner of the house next door—*my* house. He was eight or nine. He stopped when he saw me.

That was fair; I stopped when I saw him too.

I beckoned to him to come over.

He shook his head.

Slowly I walked toward him, but when I stepped off the porch the kid turned and ran away.

28

I WAS A COUPLE OF MINUTES early in the parking lot so I saw Bobbie Lee Leonard and her Rabbit as they squealed around the final corner.

She wasn't late, so she must have been hurrying just for the hell of it.

As I approached she smiled, showing a missing lower front tooth. "Mr. Samson?"

"May I see your hands, please?"

She held them up. They were much less tanned than the Frog's. Carburetors and medical bills will do that.

The nails couldn't be faulted.

"Do you want to brief me here?" she said. "Or do we have time for a cup of coffee?" She sucked air and licked her lips. I gathered she was thirsty.

"There's a snack bar in the building," I said, and led the way.

On the lot's seventh floor we crossed directly to the Bank Building's fifth, just as the Frog had on the previous Friday.

Shelley's Shop was off a corridor to the right. The tables were empty but two people stood at the counter. We waited by a bulletin board.

"This is a good one," Bobbie Lee said. 'If you eat something and nobody sees it, it has no calories.' Now, there's a philosophy of life."

I bought two coffees and we retreated to a small alcove.

"So what's the story?" she said. "I'm following this woman, right? Is it for a divorce?"

"No. For a marriage," I said. "The woman's a widow, and our client loves her. We're seeing if she's got another man in her life."

Bobbie Lee clasped her hands together before her heart. "Love," she sighed. "Sure makes the world go wrong."

I handed her the picture of Charlotte Vivien.

She studied it carefully. She said, "This widow a rich one?"

"Does it show?"

"Expensive earrings, and the blouse looks like silk," Bobbie Lee said. "And what I can see of the house suggests a decorator job."

She held the photograph for me to study. "Now you mention it," I said. I passed the picture back.

"Is your client in love with her, or is it just the money?"

"I think he has some real feeling for her."

"Lot of people are at their best dressed in dollar signs." She looked at the picture again.

"The client has no claims, but he wants to know about the opposition. The idea is to follow her, late afternoons and evenings."

She shrugged. "Is it only me? No shifts?"

"Only you. If it goes more than a few days we can review that."

"Hmm," she said. "O.K." Then, "How much is Graham charging you?"

I told her.

She did not look pleased. "You realize he's giving me less than half of that?"

"I didn't know that," I said. Then, "That doesn't seem right."

"I agreed to take less than I usually get because he spun me this tale about how you were an old friend and he was doing you a favor because your business was in a lot of trouble. Is *any* of that true?"

"No."

"Look, Mr. Samson," she began.

"If you want to bypass the man, that's all right by me as long as we log enough hours through him to make it credible."

"*Are* you some kind of friend of his?"

"Never met him before last week."

"But you want to stay in good with him?"

"I'm expanding. I'll need backup if I get more work than I can do myself. That's where Parkis comes in. Until I can start hiring people full-time."

"Mr. Samson, I think I'm in love."

"What?" I said.

She smiled big and her tongue played with the gap between her teeth. "You must have read about love."

"Uh, well . . ."

"See, I know all the licensed freelance guys on Graham's books and more. And I know who's good and who isn't and who is looking for work."

"It may be too personal a question, even to someone in love," I said, "but why haven't you set an agency up for yourself?"

"I've had one or two family complications. But it also takes money and time and that driving entrepreneurial spirit that leads guys to get in hock to the bank and advertise in the Yellow Pages." She wrinkled her nose. "Maybe someday, but not yet. And meanwhile if I can find someone to work for who isn't going to rip me off like Graham Parkis does, well, that's a guy I can stand by."

We were a couple of minutes late meeting Dancing Girl in the lobby.

Dancing Girl was not pleased. "I was about to leave," she said. "Being late is impolite of a person's time."

"I'm very sorry," I said. "But let me introduce Bobbie Lee Leonard. She is going to make the drawing from your description."

Dancing Girl spent barely a second taking in Bobbie Lee's flannel shirt, corduroy trousers and Converse Weapons. "Can we get this over with?" she said.

Once they began, however, Dancing Girl surprised me with her determination to get it right. There was a lot of give-and-take over preliminary sketches of Wool Glove Woman's clothes. Then, when Bobbie Lee brought things together on a fresh sheet of paper, Dancing Girl said, "That's it. You've got it."

"Good," Bobbie Lee said. She turned to me. "Mr. Samson, you can have this, but I'll do another drawing at home with better color, if that would help. You can have it tomorrow."

"Great," I said.

But Bobbie Lee turned back to Dancing Girl and continued to ask questions and draw. She was trying to get features of Wool Glove Woman herself from Dancing Girl's unconscious. There was certainly plenty of unconscious to work with.

The additional ten minutes didn't produce a completed image, but Dancing Girl approved a facial shape and decided on a hairstyle that didn't conflict with her memory of the woman she had talked to on Friday.

In fact, Dancing Girl was surprised that she had pulled back so much and as she studied Bobbie Lee's work she said, "The only other thing I can think of is that, for what she was, she was pretty."

"Thanks," I said. "You've been a great help."

I gave Dancing Girl more of the Scum Front's money than I had promised. She was pleased. As she left she said, "If I can help any more, you just ask, hear?"

When we were alone, Bobbie Lee asked, "What kind of case did you tell her you were working on?"

"I didn't. She didn't ask."

We looked at each other. She said, "Are you telling me *I* shouldn't ask?"

"Yup."

She shrugged, passed me a drawing and stood up. She said, "Why can't I ever fall in love with a simple man?" She headed for Charlotte Vivien.

I headed home.

WHEN I PARKED IN FRONT of my office I noticed a police car across the street. I couldn't see anything happening that required the police but there's an alley off Virginia heading east and I thought maybe that's what the cops were interested in. I didn't think it could be anything to do with me.

I took the drawing and the envelope from the Scum Front and got out of my car.

When I was halfway up my stairs I saw two people get out of the patrol car.

Since in Indianapolis patrolmen cruise solo, it seemed a little strange that two should be riding.

It seemed even stranger when they came my way.

But I went on up and into the office like the ordinary citizen I was.

Once inside, however, I allowed paranoia to trigger a frenzied gathering of the pieces of paper the Scum Front had given me. I took everything, including Bobbie Lee's drawing, and put them in the first spare room in Mom's part of the house. It was the safest instantly available place I could think of. On the way back I locked the connecting door.

I was breathing hard.

And my office bell was ringing.

I opened the door and two men stood there. One was in uniform.

"Yes?"

"Mr. Albert Samson?" The guy in plain clothes did the talking. He was about my height but heavier and he had a squashed kind of nose that hung down on his face, but with the nostrils turned up. It looked like a double-barreled ring pull.

"That's right."

"May we come in?"

"What about?"

Ring Pull practically snarled. "I got some questions to ask you. We can do it in the comfort of your own home or we can all go downtown. What's it going to be?"

"Please excuse me for insisting," I said, "but what is it about?"

"We're part of the team investigating the Scum Front, all right? We have reason to believe that you can help us with our investigation."

There was no way to keep them at bay when they invoked magic words like Scum and Front.

Ring Pull knew that. He pushed past. I shrugged in what I hoped was a convincingly casual way and said to the uniformed officer, "Well, come in."

I followed Ring Pull. The patrolman followed me.

They looked around. They didn't smile.

Ring Pull said, "I am Sergeant Ryder. This is Officer Hollenbaugh." Ryder held up some ID. But only for a moment.

I didn't ask to see it again. An excessively polite and circumspect and innocent citizen wouldn't, would he? "How can I help you?" I asked.

"You live here alone?" Ryder said.

"My office and living quarters are separate from the rest of the house. Yes, alone."

"Who lives in the other part?"

"My mother, and she has a lodger. My mother runs the luncheonette downstairs and the lodger is her griddle man."

"Uh-huh. And what do you do alone in your office, Samson?"

"I am a private detective."

"Uh-huh," Ryder said. "And what kind of work are you doing at the moment?"

"I have a few routine cases, but am also trying to increase the volume of my business."

"And how are you doing that?"

"By advertising. In fact, my first television commercial is being broadcast tonight."

"Oh yeah? When's that?"

"I don't know the exact time. The guy who made the commercial for me only got it scheduled today. He left a message on my machine. I tried to get back to him, but I couldn't."

"You sponsoring basketball games or what?"

"Uh, no. Well, I don't know. But I wouldn't think so."

I knew what was coming. It came.

"What station they on?"

"The new cable system."

"Cab-Co, huh?" He looked at me for more than a second. And he moved a step closer.

"That's it," he said.

He moved another step closer. Astonishingly, he patted my cheek with the flat of his hand. I guess he was warning me that he wasn't above making other contact.

I couldn't help myself. I took a step back.

He closed the distance between us again and had the effect of shouting by whispering in my ear, "And how did a nice guy like you get mixed up with shit bags like the Scum Front, Samson?"

My heart nearly pounded out through my eardrums. I said, "Excuse me? Mixed up with the Scum Front? Me?"

"Oh, come on. We know all about it."

And for a moment, just a moment, I felt the white-hot cut of the fear that he did.

"I am afraid," I said haltingly, "that I don't know what you are talking about."

"Book him, Hollenbaugh," Ryder said.

The patrolman moved toward me too. He said, "You know your rights, or you want me to read them to you?"

"I want to know what you're arresting me for," I said. Then, pathetically, I added, "Please."

Ryder said, "I want to know all about your connections with the Scum Front. I want to know all about your making telephone calls to Cab-Co for them." I could feel his breath and I could hardly bear it. I *wanted* to tell him all about it.

But I shook my head. "I don't understand what you're talking about."

"Oh yeah!" Ryder said with an unamused laugh.

I said, "If you ask me a clear question, I'll try to answer it."

"Last night you used a telephone."

"I use the telephone a lot." I looked to the phone on my desk. And then I remembered the tape recording I'd made of the Animals. It was still there. Oh shit!

"Not that phone," Ryder Ring Pull said. "A public phone. Now, why would a creepy private eye want to go and use a public phone when he's got a phone of his own?"

"That, frankly, is a ridiculous question," I said.

"Ridiculous, huh?" he said. "So it's ridiculous?" He slapped me.

I just backed away again.

And I could have said, "Thanks, I needed that," because it helped me regain my backbone. "When I'm in my office I use my phone. When I'm out of the office I use pay phones."

"Last night you used a telephone at Eaglegate Shopping Center."

"That's right." Then I frowned and said, "How did you know that?"

"Because your fingerprints were all over the telephone there, that's how."

I thought about the clamor of police cars roaring into the shopping center. They took prints off the phone there. Of course. How could I have made a call like that and not worn gloves!

"I leave my fingerprints on a lot of things," I said. "I don't get it."

"What were you doing at the shopping center?"

"I pulled in to get something to eat. They've got a steak house there, only when I got inside, I didn't feel like eating a steak. I came out and I called my girlfriend's house. Only she was out. Then I went into the drugstore and looked around and finally I bought a candy bar. Then I sat in the car and ate the candy bar and watched . . . Hey," I said, "there were a lot of your guys came in then. I watched all the patrol cars and, yeah, they were around the phone. Is that what this is about?"

"That's what this is about," Ryder said. "You want to get out of trouble, Samson, you think back. You want us to think it wasn't you that made the Scum Front call, how about you remember somebody else you saw that used the telephone. How about you think real hard because if you don't, then it's going to be you."

I tried to think. The only person I could think of was the woman with the sepia satin jacket in the drugstore. I nearly mentioned her, but that would have been deliberately obstructive. I shook my head. "I can't remember anybody," I said. "Sorry."

"I think you did remember somebody," Ryder said. "I seen it in your eyes."

"I remember a woman I passed a couple of words with in the drugstore. But she wasn't near the phone."

"That the kind of guy you are, Samson? Girlfriend's out and right away you're trying to pick up a replacement?"

I said nothing.

"I better have the girlfriend's name and address."

I gave them to him.

And phone number."

I gave him that. Hollenbaugh wrote it all down in his notebook.

"Right," Ryder said. "Now tell me, Samson, you been in this private detective game long?"

"Yeah. Long time."

"You haven't worked for anybody else in between? Haven't had a regular job and maybe been fired from it, something like that?"

"Nope. No regular jobs."

He took a breath. "And you didn't see anybody around the phone? Nobody at all?"

"Nobody. I wasn't near the phone long at all."

"O.K.," Ryder said. "You mind if we look around?"

I shrugged. It felt like an uncontrollable nervous tic, but maybe it didn't look that way.

Ryder went from the office into my bedroom-kitchenette. But he was gone only a few seconds. When he came back he took out a card. He said to me, "If you remember anybody or anything, give me a call."

I took the card. "Sure," I said.

"O.K.," he said. "Good." He took his first steps toward the door.

Then he stopped as if he'd thought of something. "Hey," he said. "Sorry about pushing you around a little. It's been a long day, and these people have to be found."

"I understand," I said. "No problem. All part of the job."

"Maybe if I know somebody wants a divorce I'll put him your way. You do that stuff?"

"Yeah," I said.

"Takes all kinds," he said, like he was the knight storming the citadel and I was a pile of horsecastle. "I wouldn't ever get married again myself, but Hollenbaugh here, he's going down the aisle next week, ain't that right?"

The patrolman said, "Yup."

"Unless somebody blows the church up before he gets there," Ryder said.

30

I SAT, SHAKY, FOR FIVE MINUTES.

It was all very well to tell myself, "The worst that can happen is that you go to jail," and "Worse things happen at sea," and "You've got your health." They had no therapeutic effect. Sometimes I don't listen to myself even when I shout.

But then the telephone rang. I heard *that*, But I looked at it in horror.

It kept ringing and finally the tinkle stirred me to movement. "Hello?"

There was a hesitation. "Albert?"

It was my woman, my long-suffering and much-missed woman. "Yeah," I said.

"What's wrong? You sound awful. It wasn't *that* bad. A tiny bit tacky, maybe, but effective, I thought."

"What?"

"What what?"

"What are you talking about?"

"Your commercial."

"It was on?"

"Of course it was on. What do you think, I imagined it?"

"So you saw it?"

"And heard it. And *felt* it. One of the people at work, Tina, has Cab-Co. I went over to her place, ready to sit through hours of drivel, but it came up just before seven."

"Oh, great," I said. "How was it?"

"Albert, what is the matter with you? You're talking like a zombie."

"The police were here and it's discombobulated me. Don't pay any attention."

"What did the police want?"

"They've been taking fingerprints off pay phones they think the Scum Front people might have used. I called you last night while I was out and apparently I used a phone one of *them* used."

"I told you I wasn't going to be home."

"I know. I forgot."

"Oh."

"Just one of those things."

"And the police came around about that?"

"Jerry says they are shitting bricks to get these people. Apparently when I used the phone I just missed one of them."

"Oh, how exciting," my woman said.

I felt bad about telling lies. But if there was a chance I was going to be interrogated about my movements by the police, I had to believe my lies. And if I was going to believe them I had to tell them.

"Does that mean they've left another bomb?" she asked.

"I don't know. The cops who came here didn't say."

"Anyone you know?"

"A sergeant called Ryder and a kid patrolman called Hollenbaugh who didn't say anything. I'd never seen them before."

"I don't know the names," she said. Then, "You all right otherwise?"

"I was. I am. I don't know what was wrong with me. Sorry I sounded so grim."

"Are you busy?"

"Yeah. Hey, this strange woman told me she loved me today."

"That's nice for you."

"A private eye about thirty with a missing tooth. And she knows how to fix cars."

"Sounds perfect."

"She said she loved me. But I don't know what she means by that. Hey, you know about girls. What's it mean?"

"I suppose it means she's girlish. But I only really know about women," my woman said.

There was nothing I would have liked better than to be reminded of the difference, but I needed to get in touch with an Animal. There was the minor detail of saving lives to be considered. Go-for-It Detectives have to be socially responsible.

Don't they? Didn't I read that someplace?

So it was hanky-in-the-window time. For a moment I couldn't remember where the handkerchief was. But all the Scum Front memorabilia was in Mom's part of the house.

I went through my living quarters and unlocked the door. I went into the spare bedroom.

Where I found Norman.

He was holding the drawing of Wool Glove Woman.

He was reading my messages from the Scum Front.

"What the hell do you think you're doing?" I shouted at him.

He looked up, then returned to his reading. The page on top was the list of telephone locations.

I grabbed at the papers in his hand and got the picture, which smudged a little. I snatched at the letters.

He did not resist. Instead he turned to face me, and said, "All you had to do was ask."

"What are you doing in here?"

He said, "Just who are you planning to give those to?"

"What?"

He waited, watching me with clear disdain.

He thought *I* had prepared the cut-out messages! Hang on. What did they say? About phone numbers and stuff.

I said, "That's my business."

"You're on some chickenshit case, aren't you?" He scratched himself. "Let me see. You've stolen this fashion drawing and now you're trying to sell it off without getting caught. Oh, big stuff, private eye. Looks like you're going to make your fortune this time." He shook his head slowly. "Your mother deserves better. She really does."

Which was hard for me to argue with, just at the moment. So I left it at that. I walked back to my room. I locked the door that links me to the rest of the house.

I sat and again struggled to calm myself. I contemplated the implications of my longest-ever conversation with Mom's griddle man and pistol instructor.

A few minutes later there was a knock at my door. It went through me like a fingernail on a blackboard.

I jumped out of my chair. Then I realized that the knocking was from inside the house, not outside.

I went to the door and unlocked it.

My mother stood there. She held a white handkerchief.

"Hi, Mom."

"Norman said you dropped this, son."

"Oh," I said.

"He said he thought you'd be needing it."

"Uh, yeah. I may well."

"Are you all right?"

"Fine."

"Have you got a cold, boy?"

"No."

"Flu?"

"No, Mom. I'm fine."

She held the handkerchief up, asking the silent question.

"I like to be prepared," I said. Feeble, feeble, feeble.

"Where did you get it?"

"Can't I have a handkerchief? What's the problem?"

She said slowly, "It's nice. Expensive."

"I'm not making much sense, I know. Maybe I am coming down with something."

She was not convinced. Fair enough. I was not convincing.

But before I could add to the unsatisfactoriness of the situation she said, "Have you heard from Sam lately?"

My daughter.

"No. Not for a while."

"Maybe you haven't written lately."

"Things have been busy."

"I know."

We stood for a moment.

Then she said, "If there's anything I can do for you, I will. You do know that, don't you?"

"Yes, Mom. Thanks."

"Norman's a good boy, Albert. He would help you too."

"I don't need any help, Mom."

"He would do it just because I asked him to. Whatever it was," she said. She turned and walked back down the hall to the top of the stairs.

31

I PUT THE HANDKERCHIEF in my window and tipped my gooseneck light to shine through it. I felt silly. What if a friend dropped in? How do you explain a spotlit handkerchief in your office window?

Oh well, I could say I had found religion.

I went to my desk and prepared to destroy the documents the Animals had given me.

I entered the Cab-Co number in my notebook, but with the last four digits reversed. That would fool police cryptologists.

I visualized the nine telephone locations in order. I thought I had them, but to make sure I marked them with Roman numerals on a city map.

Stupid games. Why couldn't they just give me a phone number to call in emergencies? I'd promise not to tell anybody. I'd memorize it and not write it down. Unless it was backward or upside down or something.

In a pan I burned the notes and broke up the ashes. I went into the porch and offered them up to the sweet breezes of May.

Then I came in and sat for a while. Wasn't there something useful I could be doing?

A bright white hanky in the window.

Jesus!

The telephone rang.

The sound cut me back into real life again.

"Albert Samson," I said.

A man said, "I saw your commercial tonight and I just wanted to tell you that I think you suck."

The Scum Front called a few minutes after nine.

A woman's voice said, "Three."

With a sense of real relief I took the handkerchief out of the window and headed into the night.

There was nobody using phone number three, so I stood in the hood and pretended to be looking for a number in my notebook.

I didn't do it well. I wouldn't have believed me.

On the other hand there was nobody around to perform for. So it became a philosophical question: if there is no one to lie to, is it a lie?

Well, a jerk is a jerk, that's what I say.

Wittgenstein would agree.

There was no call after six minutes.

I went back to my car and moved to telephone number four.

At this location there was major action. A man and a woman walked by arguing.

I moved on to telephone five.

Handkerchiefs!

The telephone rang.

I answered it and said, "About time."

The Bear said, "You can fuck off, Samson."

"What?"

"You're finished. I was against trusting you in the first place, you treacherous bastard. I hope you'll be able to live with yourself because any deaths are entirely your responsibility, you and your cop friends. I don't know how you did it but—" She was interrupted by a voice behind her.

I said, "I don't know what you are talking about, but I *need* to see you."

She hung up.

I stood holding the receiver for a full minute. I didn't know what had happened.

My "cop friends"?

They can't have meant Ryder and Hollenbaugh. They must know that if I was going to betray them I wouldn't invite police in the front door.

But what?

Cop friends. I didn't get it.

Finally I hung the phone up.

I went home.

There was nothing else I could do.

I put the handkerchief in the window again. It was my only link.

Then I saw there had been a telephone call while I was out.

I played the message. A pitiful male voice said that he thought his wife was cheating on him. She said she was out playing bridge with their son, but the kid was a momma's boy and might be helping to hide her infidelity. The voice asked if this was the kind of problem that I might be able to help with. It left a telephone number.

As a born-again Go-for-It Detective, was this the work I was trying so hard to drum up?

Well, maybe Bobbie Lee of the missing tooth and carburetor was about to take on another job.

I wished I still kept a whiskey bottle in my desk.

I waited by the phone into the night.

A NEW DAWNING BROUGHT the need to answer a critical question: should I contact the police and tell them what I knew?

If so, when?

If so, what?

But at eight-fifteen the decision was taken out of my hands. The police, in the form of Jerry Miller, called me. He said, "Al, there's something I'd like to talk to you about. Do you think you could come down and see me?"

"What, you mean like lunch?"

"Before lunch. This morning. Now."

"Has something happened, Jerry?"

"No, no," he said without conviction. "I would just like to have a little talk. What time do you think you can get down here?"

A little after ten-thirty his secretary waved me straight through to his office.

"O.K., sport," I said. "What the hell is going on?"

"Sit down," he said.

He had the same air of reserve that he'd had on the phone and I thought about battling him all the way down the line. But I didn't have a clue what it was about. It might be personal. It might be that he had decided to leave Janie at last and he wanted help with his farewell letter.

I sat down.

"He said, "We have briefings first thing these days."

I waited.

"Scum Front," he said.

I waited silently again, but this time because I couldn't have said anything if I'd wanted to.

He said, "Reviewing. You know. What guys did yesterday on the case. Latest pronouncements from on high. And this morning, Al, you can imagine what I felt when I caught *your* name."

I nodded and swallowed and tried to locate my voice. "I . . . I had a couple of guys come around."

"So I read," Miller said. He picked up some papers from his desk. But he didn't look at them. He looked at me. "Anyhow, so when I heard the name I asked Ryder for his report."

I went for "injured innocent." "What's the problem?"

Miller didn't answer the question. He waved the papers slowly. "You made a call from a public phone, right?"

"Right."

"To—"

"Only she was out. What *is* the problem, Jerry?"

"Well, I don't know if you know, there's a new gadget available on phones."

"Is this going to take long? Because I've got a young daughter and I don't want to miss her fiftieth birthday party."

"When we get a call in the department, this gadget automatically gives us the source telephone number and the location of the phone the call is being made from."

I waited.

"The information goes on a rolling computer thing so we keep records for thirty-six hours before they get wiped to be replaced by the new calls. The same equipment can be put on other phones and because of the importance of the Scum Front case we've got all the pay phones in central Indianapolis hooked up. The Scummies use them to call Cab-Co."

"Jerry, I know about that. I saw it in action. I was sitting in my car dealing with some serious calories and I saw cops coming out of the woodwork to get at that phone in the shopping center."

"Yeah, but maybe you didn't know that the equipment also records the time the calls are made."

"Yeah? So?"

"Well, when I looked at Ryder's file on you it included a copy of the calls made at the phone in question."

"Jerry, the point!"

He sighed and said, "Two things bothered me, Al. I can't quite believe what I'm thinking, but I can't shake them either."

"What, for Christ's sake?"

"First, there's the call you said you made."

"It's there, isn't it?"

"Oh yeah. It's here. But the problem is the time." He looked at me. "It's nineteen minutes before the Scum Front call to Cab-Co."

"So?"

"So you told Ryder—and me just now—that you saw patrol officers come into the shopping center and seal off the phone. You watched them from your car while you ate a chocolate bar."

"Yeah. So?"

"But it also says here that you didn't see anybody use the phone."

"Your reading's come on a lot. Soon they'll let you start the Dick and Jane book where Spot does dirty things with his ball."

"See, the picture I get," he persisted, "is that you're in your car able to watch our guys around the phone a few minutes after a Scummie uses it, but somehow you didn't see anybody at the phone or near it before then."

"What am I supposed to do? Make it up? If you'd told me

I was supposed to devote my attention to a phone booth I would have done it."

"Could you do me a favor, Al? Could you draw me a little sketch of the parking lot and where you were parked and where the phone was and where you got the candy from?"

"Yeah, I could do that. But why should I? All you're doing is saying you don't believe me when I say I can notice cops screaming into a mall but I can fail to notice somebody putting a quarter in a slot."

"You're a trained observer, Al."

"I guess I forgot to take my field glasses. But *am* I supposed to make it up? O.K. I saw a seven-foot guy in a Pacers uniform dribbling something round that had wires sticking out and ticked."

"No, of course you aren't supposed to make things up."

"Well, what's your problem, then? Do you think *I'm* a Scum Fronter?"

"Nooo," he said, like with two-percent "maybe" in it. "But you're not the most contented member of our community."

"I'll moo for you."

"It's not a joke, Al."

"O.K. It's not a joke. So tell me this. Suppose I am involved with the Scum Front. Do you think I would be so stupid as to make a call for them and leave my fingerprints?"

He shrugged.

"I do know about fingerprints, Jerry. They've been around for a long time. Even Mark Twain knew about fingerprints."

"And there's this other thing," he said.

"You better say it quick, before I get into trouble for assaulting a police officer."

"You don't like being pushed around like this, do you?"

"No, I don't."

"Well, Ryder has this rep," Miller said.

"Congratulate him for me."

"He's abrasive. He's not polite. We get complaints on him. Everybody knows about Ryder. There are jokes. There's a break-in at a church where the minister is ninety years old, people say, 'Send Ryder. He'll get a confession.'"

"So?"

"In his report," Miller said, "Ryder said how cooperative you'd been with him, Al. And I asked him myself, and he said the same. 'All please and thank you' was how he described you."

Miller and I looked at each other.

Miller said, "A cop comes to your door. This is a cop who thinks he's too important for routine work. This is a cop who once broke the skull of a drunk who didn't call him 'Sir.' He comes to your door and he interrupts whatever you are doing and he takes up your time asking about a phone call you made that is none of his business. Undoubtedly he shouts at you to put you under stress to see if you act like a terrorist. Maybe he roughs you up a little. Probably he noses around your place. And you, Al, you do not take his badge number. You do not make sarcastic cracks that show him up for the asshole he most certainly is. You do not refuse to answer his questions. You talk to the guy and play it his way and nod and smile and say how you know he's just doing his job. And that, Albert, is just not like you. You eat situations like this with a brown-sugar topping. The better mood you're in, the more of a meal you make out of it. It's fun to guys like you. But, for some reason, not this time. This time you're smiles and sunshine and 'all please and thank you.' So I ask myself why. And I ask you, why, Al? *Why?*"

I GOT OUT OF POLICE headquarters without wearing handcuffs. What I did wear was guilt and a distinct sense of the world closing in on me.

I put it back on Miller. He and I had lunched, right? He'd bellyached about how the Scum Front stuff was eating away at the morale of the police department. Then—strictly coincidentally—my prints had come up and a cop came around. It would have been actively obstructive, quite apart from simply stupid, to give a cop a hard time in circumstances like that. Even a bad cop. Right?

Don't I know the difference between something serious and something I can joke about?

Wasn't the fact that Miller was giving me a hard time evidence that I was right to take Ryder's crap, because the Scum Front was driving all cops crazy? If I'd made a crack with Ryder he'd probably have shot me.

Right?

I wore Miller down. Eventually he began to realize that

what he'd thought of as a perception was actually the mental aberration of a restless policeman whose home life was nearly as complicated as his professional life.

And once I got him onto Janie, I was in the clear. Before I left he told me a joke that was circulating in the department: what is the difference between a wife and a terrorist?

"I don't know, Jerry. What *is* the difference between a wife and a terrorist?"

"You can negotiate with a terrorist."

I laughed for him.

On the answering machine there was a message from Bobbie Lee. She asked when and how I would like to take possession of the color version of her drawing.

I called back immediately. I got her answering machine, who coughed to clear her throat and sounded about eighty. She said, "Bobbie Lee is not to home just now. You want to leave a message, I'll tell her soon as she sets foot inside the door. I got a pencil."

I left my name and suggested that Bobbie Lee might come by my office on the way to her evening assignment.

And I thanked the machine, who said, "Oh, 'tain't no problem," and then hung up.

I sat in my chair for a minute and doodled to see if I could think about what I should be doing. But brain activity was an uncomfortable process and my doodles were all dress-shaped and faceless.

I went outside, down the stairs and around to the luncheon-ette. It was early for lunch. I ordered food anyway.

But not the chili. I needed all the love I could get.

While Norman poked at my cooking food as if it were already me, I played the pinball machine.

When he slapped the plate on the counter I lost my final ball. I ate in silence and left a ten-cent tip.

* * *

On the way back upstairs my brain made its play. I decided to put the hanky in the window again and give it an hour. If there was no call I would go out to Cecil Redman's house and try to make some progress there.

TWO LITTLE GIRLS WERE playing with an empty three-wheeled baby carriage in front of Cecil Redman's house.

It was a kind of dare. The kids stood several feet apart on the sidewalk and took turns pushing the vehicle at each other as hard as they could. Could you hang on to it and not fall down? Were you brave enough not to jump out of the way? The carriage's eccentric motion was the wild card and sent them both into fits of giggles. Only a thin strip of grass between the sidewalk and the street kept the shuttle from coming under traffic regulations. It was vigorous, funny, dangerous kid stuff and I wanted to play.

But the modern Go-for-It Detective doesn't get to play games just any old time he feels like it. Instead he goes to front doors and plays games of his own.

My knocks were answered by a short woman with glossy cheeks and bright eyes who looked up at me as if she had answered doors belligerently all her born life. "What you want?" she inquired.

"Is Cecil Redman here, please?"

"What for you want Cecil?"

"I want to talk to him about something."

"He ain't done nothing."

"I just think he can help me."

"If he do, you be the first."

"Is he around?"

"No, he ain't 'around'."

"Do you know where he is?"

"Could be."

I smiled. "I'm not a cop."

"I know you ain't a cop," she said. "You too squishy soft the way you talk for a cop. You more like a . . ." She studied me with a practiced eye. "You more like a cyclopedia salesman."

"Thanks a lot."

"He ain't buying nothing."

"I ain't selling nothing."

She closed one eye and half smiled and said, "Or maybe you a runner for the numbers. Somebody do you a favor and give you the job, you promise to stay off the booze. Somebody knew your poppa."

"I wish I was half that interesting."

She studied me again and decided. "You know the club?" she asked.

"What club?"

"Ain't no real club. But it ain't no headquarters neither."

"No?"

"What goes on there has more to do with the other end."

"Excuse me?"

"You don't get it, do you?"

"No."

"They calls it a *head* quarters."

"Ah, ah."

"You stupid, huh? Well, you better *join* the club."

The woman stepped out onto the porch and pointed down the street. "It be a little white building over 24th Street, other side of Illinois. They got a sign on it say 'HQ.' They do all their plottin' and plannin' in there."

"And he's likely to be there?"

"That's what I said, ain't it?" She shook her head a couple of times and turned her back on me.

The pickup truck was parked in front of "HQ." The building had once been a little grocery, according to the remains of advertising on the wall. But it was clear that, like so many of the others in the area, it had long been neglected.

Yet now it was being used. In black paint below the roof there were big letters and little letters. The big letters read "HQ Club." The little letters read, "H-elp save our Q-uarters."

I could hear men talking inside.

I knocked on the piece of wood that had replaced the glass in the door.

The talking stopped. But nothing else happened.

I knocked again and I heard footsteps.

The door opened and a huge man frowned down at me. He said, "Now, what is all the racket about?"

"Sorry to bother you," I said, "but I was told I could find Cecil Redman here."

The man's expression did not change as he turned slightly and called inside. "Cecil. Looks like you been forgetting to pay your liquor bills again."

Without moving his head, the man winked the eye closer to me.

From inside I heard, "Say what?" Also some quiet laughter.

"Man here wants you, Cecil. He looks mean as hell."

"Aw shit."

The huge man said to me, "You coming in, or what?"

I went in.

The room was dark. Though there were a couple of candles burning on shelves, the main light came from foot-wide gaps above the boards in the side windows.

There were two card tables in the middle of the room and they supported sheets of paper and empty beer cans in equal numbers. Along one wall another table bore a mimeograph machine. In the middle stood a kerosene stove, but it did not seem to be on. At the back there was a door, but from the size of the whole building it couldn't have led to anything bigger than a closet or a toilet.

Near the door an empty chair clearly belonged to my "host." Half a dozen other unopened folding chairs leaned against walls. Two more chairs near the card tables were occupied. Both men were black. One was thin and wiry. The other, a bald man wearing a lumber jacket, was even bigger than the large white man who had opened the door to me. From the Bear's description, Cecil Redman had to be the wiry guy.

Redman wore a floppy cloth cap that I recognized as green because it happened to be in a shaft of light. He squinted at me as I came in. "What you want about some goddamned liquor bill? I don't owe no liquor bill."

"I'm not a debt collector," I said.

"So what you be?" he asked.

This question seemed to be of interest to all the men. The six eyes suddenly felt weighty.

I had considered a couple of stories—lies—I could tell if I found Redman. But under the pressure of close scrutiny I decided to settle for a truth. "I'm a private detective," I said.

Redman's cheeks rose with displeasure. "Say what?" He turned away. "Aw shit," he said.

The other men exchanged smiles and the lumberjack said, "Told you, Cecil. Didn't I tell you she a mean black devil bitch? Didn't I say? Didn't I say?"

My host said, "She's gonna get you, Cecil. She's gonna get you. Thousand bucks a week, minimum."

Redman jumped up and faced me. "I ain't got no money. You ask my club members here. I ain't got money. You and the bitch can take me to jail but it ain't gonna get blood out of my stone." He turned to his friends in turn. "Have I got money? Have I got money?"

Neither man said anything at first but then the lumberjack said, "Except for the stash of cash under your bed."

My host's hoots of laughter drowned out what I lip-read Cecil to be saying. In a fit of frustration, he overturned one of the tables. Beer cans rattled like machine-gun fire and a few sheets of paper hovered in the air and landed on the cans. Redman's gesture did not quiet his colleagues or appear to concern them.

I bent to pick up the papers. My host righted the table. And Cecil sat down.

It seemed a good time for me to speak. I said, "I'm not here representing anybody who is trying to get money out of you."

I guess I have more stage presence than I realized. Everyone fell silent.

Redman said, "Well, what you want, then?"

"Do you remember, beginning of February, seeing four women with suitcases?"

The big men continued to study me. Cecil said, "Suitcases? Man, what you on at me about suitcases?"

"Behind an empty house, just north of 23rd Street."

"There a lot of empty houses round here," he said. "That's what we fighting."

"We? You mean the club?"

"Action group," the lumberjack said. "We are an action group."

My host asked, "Where do you live, mister?"

"South side. Virginia Avenue."

"Wait till the money guys get it in their pretty little heads to push out that way. You see how you like it they take your goddamned house and make it a zoo or an Inner Loop or a IUPUI."

The acronym for Indiana University and Purdue University at Indianapolis is pronounced "youie pooie." It was not said with affection.

"The gentrifiers are out my way now," I said. "I live near Fountain Square."

"So you know what we're talking about," my host said.

"I know about not having a place of my own, but I don't understand why all the houses around here are empty or why they've been empty for so long."

"Because the people who lived in them all their lives are too poor to be permitted to stay in them now downtown's being fixed up, that's why," my host said.

"They make us a historical area," the lumberjack said.

"And our places get condemned," Redman said.

"And then the pretty boys come in and fix up our houses and make all the money," my host said.

The lumberjack said, "But we working on it, man."

"How?"

"We got ways," he said.

My host was more forthcoming. He said, "We track down who owns the buildings and what the plans are for them. We write letters saying how people need places to live. We talk to folks in the neighborhoods. We do leaflets and stuff."

I looked at the mimeograph machine and then looked back at the three men in their candlelit room.

The lumberjack said, "Don't underestimate what the little man can do if he tries. My daddy was down Montgomery and he told me how all that happened."

I didn't know what he meant.

"You think the bus boycotts come from admen and TV commercials?"

"Of course not."

"I tell you how that happened, man. That happened because when Rosa Parks got arrested for being too damn tired to give up her seat on the bus to some damn white man, there was guys like us down there got mad about it, that's how."

Redman and my host nodded.

"Them guys run some leaflets off and started spreading them around and it was them leaflets said, 'Boycott the buses.' That's where it started, it sure did."

"I see," I said.

"Oh no, you don't," he said. "There wasn't but a hundred leaflets. Ain't no way a few itty-bitty pieces of paper going to start the Montgomery bus boycotts that led Reverend Martin Luther King, Jr., to international significance and got civil rights going, now is there? Not all by themselves."

"Well . . ."

"No, there ain't. But what happened down there was this. Some of them leaflets got dropped on the sidewalk and in the gutter and there they was, laying around. And what happened was some guy picks one up and says to himself, 'Shit, man, them damn niggers is going to boycott the buses!' And this guy, he runs off to the Sunday newspaper and they print this big story threatening all the bad things going to happen to the niggers if they do try a boycott."

"Ah," I said.

"And what happens then is that all the preachers sit down to their grits and collard greens and shit on Sunday morning and they read about the boycott in the paper. Only they didn't know nothing about it before. But they do now and they go out to their pulpits and say to all the folks in church, they say, 'You go boycott the buses, if you want to. You go use your feet to lead us to freedom.' That's what they said and that's what they did and that's the truth. So don't you look around here and say to yourself, these guys can't change nothing. Because we can. And we will."

"O.K.," I said. "You've made the point."

"All right!" the lumberjack said. He slapped his knee. His two colleagues echoed him. "All right!" "All right!"

I nodded.

Then my host said slowly, "Which still don't sort out just who you are and what you want."

I pulled out my license card and showed them. "I'm a private detective. I've been hired by one of the four women with the suitcases I mentioned. She noticed Cecil watching them and took down the plate number on his pickup."

"Aw shit," Redman said.

"Then this woman thought that she saw Cecil again and that got her worried and she thought about it and finally she's hired me to find out what Cecil was doing hanging around. And that's it." And that *was* it, more or less.

I said to Redman, "Do you remember those women with the suitcases?"

"Aw shit," he said again.

"Did you recognize any of them?"

"Rich bitch white women come walking around down here? How the hell am I supposed to recognize one?"

"But then she saw you hanging around."

"Aw shit," Cecil said. "Aw shit. It against the law to stand outside a house?"

"So you do know one of them?"

I tried not to sound too excited.

"I don't *know* people like that!" he said, but he was fidgeting and uncomfortable. "I did kind of remember this one bitch and she reminded me of something."

"What she remind you of, Cecil?" the lumberjack asked. He was readier than my host to move on to a little sounding. "What she remind you of? Something you ain't had for so long you almost forgot what it is?"

Cecil said, "Aw shit."

"So you followed her?" I said.

"No I didn't follow her, man. I didn't need to follow nobody. I knew where she lived."

"How?"

"'Cause," he said, looking from one of his colleagues to the other, "'cause my old lady's momma clean for that woman's family most her life, that's how."

"Your old lady?"

"My wife, man."

"The one you thought had hired me?"

"How many wives you think I got?" he said, his face expressing pain.

The lumberjack said, "He gotta keep him a list. He gotta count on his fingers."

"Aw shit," Redman said as the other two enjoyed his discomfort. But then he said, "So seeing this white woman reminded me, like I hadn't seen Louanne for a long time."

"He think she miss him sooo bad," the lumberjack said.

This time Redman joined in the laughter. He pointed to me. "Well, the man told you it was February. I thought I'd take her a goddamn valentine."

"A valentine?" my host asked.

"Man, women like all that shit."

"But Louanne's too smart to fall for that, isn't she?"

"She's a smart woman—"

"Now she rid of you," the lumberjack said.

"Yeah, well, maybe so. But she still got her moods. My

Louanne may have her a pair of brass balls but she always go soft as mush for valentines and that stuff."

I said, "But if it was Louanne you wanted to see, why did you go to the white woman's house?"

"'Cause I didn't know where Louanne live. So I gonna ask Momma."

"What you give Momma in exchange?" the lumberjack said.

But Cecil said, "What that white woman think I'm doing there? Waiting to rob her or something? Shit. I ain't no goddamn thief."

I said, "So, what's the name of the woman your wife's mother works for?"

"Man, I don't remember no goddamned name."

"But you know where her house is."

"Yeah. Louanne fill in sometimes for Momma and I picked her up once or twice."

"So where is the house?"

"Big brick place up on 91st Street."

"You know the number?"

"No I don't know no goddamned number but I go up College and turn west and there ain't but one with this big iron fence all around it."

I nodded, trying to look casual about having been told where a member of the Scum Front lived.

But the big man who had opened the door to me suddenly frowned and said, "Hey."

It was a hostile noise and everybody was surprised by it.

"Tell me something, mister," he said.

"Yeah?"

"If you're a private eye investigating for some woman, how come you got to ask *him* what the woman's name is and where she lives?"

It was a reasonable question.

It was an awkward moment.

I said, "Come on, man. It's part of my job. I have to check and make sure *he's* talking about the same woman and the same house I am, don't I?"

* * *

I stayed a while longer with the HQs and before I left I asked if I could make a financial contribution to their cause. Maybe a donation about the size of the cost of a case of beer.

"Hey," the lumberjack said, "Christmas done gone and come round again already."

I had found where the Frog lived! I was very pleased with myself as I turned onto College at 25th Street. On the opposite corner a hand-painted sign offered me "Buffalo, 99¢/lb," but I declined and headed north toward 91st.

I had the drive to consider what I would do when I got there. But no way was I not going to have a look.

35

COLLEGE AVENUE IS A PRIMER for the neighborhood changes on the north side. From the interstate that is part of the Inner Loop up to Fall Creek, College is one of the most decimated streets of the rubble belt. On each block there are empty houses, stores or schools. The area's atmosphere of abandonment is inescapable.

Once across Fall Creek—about 28th Street—the tone changes. This neighborhood used to be "white" but now the blacks uprooted by the development and yuppification downtown have filled it. This shift has caused a knock-on exodus, neighborhood by neighborhood. But the farther north you go, the higher the prices get and that slows change. By 49th Street you have a "Kitchens of Distinction." The first "pub" is at the corner of 52nd.

After that Broad Ripple is Indianapolis's artsy-craftsy area and it remains the only part of the city where a mixed-race couple can walk hand in hand with a chance of not being hassled.

College crosses the canal before you hit the first condos,

and White River before there are residential areas with private security patrols.

By the time I turned west on 91st Street I had driven seven miles and was almost at the city line.

I was also approaching a decision. The closer I got to the Frog's house, the less comfortable I had become. Looking at a house is not a one-way phenomenon.

The resident of the house might look back.

So before I went very far on 91st I pulled over.

Was I ready to let the Scum Front know that I had cracked their security? If the Frog was walking her Rottweiler or scolding her gardener or even just counting money in the window and she happened to look up . . .

What then?

I couldn't figure out what criteria to apply to make decisions.

My unease skipped agitation and went straight to panic when a police car pulled up behind me.

36

THE PATROL OFFICER WAS a woman about five four.

For an instant I thought about driving away. Running.

I touched the key in my ignition.

But why? What from?

I closed my eyes and could barely hear myself think from the noise of my breathing.

But I heard her tap on my window clear enough.

I rolled it down and said, "Is there a problem, Officer?"

"Would you mind stepping out, sir?"

I didn't move at first.

She said, "Outside the car, please, sir."

I opened the door and moved to get out. It was hard. My muscles were on a slowdown. Finally I made it. I leaned against the car. I felt faint.

"Are you all right?"

"I feel faint," I said.

"You look awful," she said.

"I was driving along and I didn't feel good so I pulled over."

She studied me. I was sure she knew I was lying. I

thought that—somehow—she knew everything. I wanted to drop to my knees and beg forgiveness.

She moved forward. I would have settled for just dropping to my knees. But she took my left hand and felt for a pulse. "Heart's beating pretty fast," she said.

"I know."

"You hurt anyplace?"

Only in my brain. "I have a headache."

"No chest pains?"

"No."

"Left arm feel normal?"

Absurdly I felt it with my right hand. "Yeah," I said. "I'm all right. I'll be all right."

"Have you felt faint before?"

"Once or twice. But I'm going to see my doctor."

"You should," she said. Then she seemed to get an idea. "You haven't been drinking, have you, sir?"

"Drinking? Oh. Alcohol. No. No. Nothing to drink."

"Would you mind standing away from the car for a moment?"

I moved away from the car.

"Lift your right leg and hold it."

"Hold it with what?"

"Hold it up, sir."

"Ah." I did it. Then the left. I said, "I am sober. No booze. No drugs. No rock and roll. I just felt faint."

She nodded, but she looked closely at my eyes.

I guess they were both still there because then she said, "Come back here a minute, will you, sir?"

She walked toward the rear of my car. I followed. "See," she said. "Tire's right down."

I saw.

"I didn't know whether you knew," she said. "That's why I stopped."

"I didn't know. Thanks. I have a foot pump in the trunk."

"Get it out, will you, sir?"

"Excuse me?"

"Get your foot pump out, please."

I got it out.

She took it from me. "If you're feeling faint, you shouldn't do anything strenuous," she said. And she pumped the tire up.

When she drove away I felt relieved, even elated. I got in the car, started it and pulled back into traffic.

In less than a minute I saw the house that Cecil Redman had described. It was set back from the road, and the property was surrounded by wrought-iron fencing. But the iron gates hanging from red brick pillars were open.

I drove in.

I was a Go-for-It Detective as seen on TV. Right?

NO ONE ANSWERED THE bell at first. But as my finger was poised to ring it again, the door opened.

I don't know what I was expecting. I got a seven-year-old boy.

"I'm sick," he said.

I offered a hand. "How do you do, Sick?"

He shook it and at the same time he turned away and giggled.

"Is . . . is your mother at home?"

"Yup."

When there was no advance on "yup" I said, "Sick, do you think you could get her for me?"

He nodded and ran through a double doorway at the back and right of the house.

I stepped inside.

From out of sight I heard, "Mom. Mom. There's a man and he called me sick!"

After a few moments a woman appeared in the doorway where Sick had disappeared. She didn't look up as she moved my way because Sick was swinging on a fistful of her sweatsuit pants and pulling them down. At the same time the woman was wiping her hands on a paper towel. She was five feet tall, had curly dark blond hair and she moved with even, balanced steps. She wore an apron covered in tiny hearts. Each hand had two rings.

When finally she raised her eyes to me, she stopped as if shot.

I had never seen her face. But it was the Frog.

No doubt.

She was only shot for a moment. She said, "Can I help you?"

"I think you can," I said.

"Are . . . are you selling something? Or what?"

"You know perfectly well who I am," I said.

"I'm sorry. I think you may have confused the address with . . . Well, I don't know."

"Mom," Sick said. "Are you done with the bowl yet?"

She shushed him and he burrowed poutily between her legs.

I smiled and said, "I guess maybe he isn't that sick after all."

"Yes, I am," he said without appearing. "I am too sick."

I said, "I'm not here to cause trouble. But I need to see you people."

"What people, Mom?"

"I don't know what you mean," the Frog said.

To help her avoid Sick's interventions I spoke in a foreign language: big words. I said, "Number one. I have not, repeat not, communicated anything substantive to members of local law enforcement agencies. Not yet. Number two. I have located a witness who confirms that someone followed you in the downtown building we have spoken of. My witness helped an artist make á likeness. I need members of your special interest group to look at that likeness so that I—we—can progress. But suddenly nobody answers my hanky."

The little pitcher stepped out and pointed a finger at me. He said, "You're silly. Nobody *answers* a hanky. Hankies don't talk!"

I nodded. "Sick," I said, "you are absolutely right."

"I know," he said.

"I *am* silly. Very, very silly," I said. "That's because I have this trusting nature that makes me believe people when they say their social responsibilities are important to them. I even believe people when they say they want to correct their mistakes. My trusting nature gets me into trouble. But there comes a time when even I learn better. And then I take the straightest line to get myself out of the deep doodoo that other people have put me in."

"Mom, he said 'doodoo'!"

"It's all right," she said.

I said, "I'm at my limit, Mom. Somebody better give me a telecommunication later on today. And I don't mean an I Spy call. Somebody better be ready to talk English and make arrangements. We need to coalesce to examine my artist's impression. We need to engage in a little verbal interaction. *Capisce?*"

IT WAS A QUARTER TO FIVE when I got back to my office. I felt exhausted. I'd been in too many intense situations in too few days.

Don't get me wrong. I can do emotion. I'm not a frozen cabbage. But it costs me and after a while even an emotional high roller is going to bottom out.

I went up the stairs slowly and with some trepidation. Too often of late coming home meant Quentin Quayle or the cops or Norman or . . .

This time, however, the surprise was on the answering machine. In my absence there had been seven calls. But that wasn't it. The surprise was that not a single message was from anybody I knew. They were all from people who wanted to talk about possible work. Five different people. They sought appointments. One had called three times.

I replayed the messages and listed names and numbers in my notebook. It was hard to believe.

Maybe I shouldn't believe it. Maybe it was somebody's idea of a joke.

But maybe it wasn't. And any excuse to hope for an

orderly future and a life without dress-up bombers and moody British poets was positively welcome.

So I made a positive move. I left my door unlocked, stuck a note to Bobbie Lee on it and took a very hot shower.

It was wonderful. It ranked in my top ten lifetime physical feelings, an all-singeing, all-drenching, all-body experience. I came out pink and young again. As I dried myself I hummed.

I dressed in crisp clean clothes. That felt good too.

It was five twenty-five when I came back into my office.

Bobbie Lee was not only there, she was sitting at my desk with her feet up. She was thumbing through my notebook. She said "So this is what it's like to be a hotshot detective."

"You like the sensation?"

"I think I'd get a better chair. One of those lean-back jobs that support your head."

"I'll try to remember that when I'm choosing a present for your agency opening."

In a voice that reminded me immediately of Graham Parkis she said, "Do sit down, young man. Now let's hear all about this sexual perversion you think your wife is getting up to with the Cub Scout who mows your grass."

I said, "I can see you have the gift of a deskside manner."

"I am a gold mine waiting to be discovered," she said. Then, "Would you like your life back?"

Without waiting for an answer she shifted her feet to the floor, rose and dropped my notebook with a plop.

"Thanks," I said.

"I've got a picture for you and I've got a report. Which do you want first?"

"Let's have the picture."

Her folder was on the desk. She opened it and turned a color drawing of a woman toward me.

"It's in chalks but I've sprayed them so it won't smudge."

The drawing of Wool Glove Woman was much more vivid than the sketch in pencils had been. "I'm impressed," I said.

"If you find her, maybe you could ask if she wants a formal portrait. I'm very reasonable."

I smiled.

She said, "The clothes are right. The face is less reliable. As you know, the witness didn't have an eye for people."

"I've got some clients coming to take a look at it later tonight."

"You seem to have a lot of clients," she said. She gestured toward the notebook. "If you need some help . . ."

"Whatever I can put your way, Ms Leonard, I will."

"My report," she announced. She pulled out a notebook of her own. "I engaged the target as she left her residence at nineteen forty-nine hours."

"We speak English here."

"Then I lost the target at twenty thirty-one."

"Lost her? After forty-two minutes?"

"Correct."

"How?"

"I think 'Why?' would be a better question."

"O.K. Why?"

"Because the other guy following her doesn't know shit about how to do it."

"Someone else followed her?"

Bobbie Lee nodded. "A popular gal, your Mrs. Vivien."

I didn't know what to make of it.

She said, "As soon as she spotted the other guy we did one-way streets and a couple of alleys and burned some rubber. It was all very exciting for at least four minutes."

"Did you get a look at him?"

"I did better than that. I took his picture. But I didn't know whether I was supposed to keep with the target and let the guy know I was there or whether it was better for me to be discreet, but lose her. My inclination was to run him off the road. But since I was working for you, and since my own inclinations tend to get me into trouble, and since I figured if she was looking for tails, that was going to make it almost impossible for me by myself anyway . . . I decided not to take chances without further instructions. There wasn't time to call in. Besides, pal, you told me it was going to be easy."

"I thought it would be," I said. "I wouldn't lie to you, Bobbie Lee."

She laughed.

"You've heard that before, huh?"

"A hundred times before I decided to give up men."

"A hundred!" I said.

She laughed again. It was easy, appealing laughter.

I said, "Let's see the picture of the guy."

From beneath her drawing she pulled out a photograph. She laid it on the desk in front of me.

It was shadowy and grainy. It was also George Quentin Crispian Quayle.

"Oh shit," I said.

"Who is it? CIA? KGB? IRS?"

"It is," I said, "our client."

"Oh," she said.

"He's a real jerk," I said.

And then the doorbell rang.

QUAYLE LOOKED UNHAPPY. "I've come by four times today," he said.

"A detective's work is never done. Believe me, running a twenty-four-hour car wash single-handed would be a rest cure."

"What?"

"Come in, Poet," I said. "There's someone I want you to meet."

Quayle sulked in.

But he transformed himself when he saw a young woman in the room.

Bobbie Lee extended a hand. "I'm Bobbie Lee Leonard," she said.

Quayle took the hand in both of his and lifted it to his mouth. He not only kissed it but he lingered in the process. He said, "It is an enchanting pleasure to meet you. I am Quentin C. Quayle."

"I've never had my hand kissed before," she said.

"I am a connoisseur of hands and since I arrived on your shores I have not grasped a more exquisite one."

"You're English, huh?"

"I have that good fortune. And do I presume too much if I surmise that you, Ms Leonard, are Hoosier?"

"Born and bred."

"You have the quality of carriage and bearing that I have come to associate with the genuine Hoosier woman. In fact I venture to suggest that Hoosier womanhood can stand up against the womanhood of any other persuasion."

"Probably knock them down again too," Bobbie Lee said.

"But with style and verve."

"Yeah. We go in a lot for verve. But if the verve ain't gettin' the job done, then we break off a high hard one."

I said, "I hate to pour disinfectant on this exchange of cow patter, but Ms Leonard has some work to do."

"She works?" Quayle said. "This creature works?"

Bobbie Lee could not suppress a chuckle.

"She works for you, Poet."

He caused his jaw to drop and his eyebrows to lift.

"She's following Charlotte Vivien."

"Oh," he said. He looked at her again.

"Want to start over? Hi. I'm Bobbie Lee Leonard." She extended her hand.

Quayle said, "She's a detective?"

"Right first time."

"Gee," Bobbie Lee said, "I hoped you were going to slobber on it again. A little more and I could throw my moisturizer away."

"However," I said, "her work last night was not helped by your getting in the way."

"What do you mean?" Quayle asked.

Bobbie Lee went to my desk and picked up the photograph she'd taken of him. "I followed the target last night but this man was following her too. She spotted him and shook him and that meant that I couldn't stay with her."

"Oh," Quentin Quayle said.

"The point, Poet, is that you either leave the job to us or you do it yourself. They are mutually exclusive options. It is time for Ms Leonard to leave. Do you want Mrs. Vivien followed or not?"

"I do. I do," he said. But he had hardly taken his eyes off Bobbie Lee since they were introduced.

"Then whatever else you get up to tonight, do not follow Mrs. Vivien again yourself."

Quentin Quayle looked from Bobbie Lee to me and back. "Couldn't I go along with her?"

"Don't be ridiculous."

"I don't mind," Bobbie Lee said.

"You must be joking."

"At least that way I know where he is."

"It's unprofessional," I said.

And then I wondered if that was really what I was responding to.

"It *is* my money," Quayle said.

I said to Bobbie Lee, "Are you seriously suggesting that he rides with you?"

"If he weighs the car down too much in a high-speed chase I can always dump him. In fact I know a block where all the transvestite hookers hang out. It'd take him hours to kiss his way through all the beautiful hands down there."

Poet's pupils dilated further.

I shrugged. The Go-for-It Detective was dead; long live the Laid-back Go-for-It Detective.

Quayle reached for the photograph of himself. "May I keep that?"

"Sure," Bobbie Lee said.

Then Quayle pointed to the desk. "Can I have that too?"

"My desk? Certainly not."

"The other picture. Can I have it?"

He meant the color chalk drawing of Wool Glove Woman. "No," I said. "That's nothing to do with you."

"What do you mean it's nothing to do with me?" he said. "That's one of Charlotte's dresses."

I looked at him. I was so surprised I couldn't speak.

BOBBIE LEE SAW MY reaction. She said, "Are you saying it's like a dress you are familiar with, Mr. Quayle?"

"It's not *like* it. It *is* it. Charlotte wore that dress when we went to a party in January. I'd recognize it anywhere."

His intensity of feeling grew and Bobbie Lee and I exchanged glances.

Quayle began to wave his hands and said, "I am a poet. An artist. My eyes are tools. People burn themselves into my brain and bring their garments with them. I know clothes, Ms Leonard. You, for instance, are a perfect ten. The dress in that drawing was designer-made as an approximate twelve but taken in at the waist. Charlotte has exceptionally slender hips for a woman of her height."

Bobbie Lee did not respond and Quayle turned to me. "You know her, Samson. Do you think that a woman like Charlotte Vivien buys her dresses from a Sears Roebuck catalog? Each of her garments is unique. That dress *is* one of Charlotte's. And I want to know what you are doing with a drawing of it on your desk."

"You're not my only client," I said.

"What is that supposed to mean?"

"This happens to be one of a series of drawings for a fashion company."

"What fashion company? In Indianapolis?"

"That is not your business."

"What do *you* do for a fashion company?"

"I get them drawings of garments that they might not see otherwise."

"You steal designs? Oh, Albert, I am disappointed."

"I'm not admitting to anything illegal. But look at the picture. There's almost no face at all."

"Yes," he said slowly.

"Which proves it's a fashion drawing," I said. "It is the clothes that are important."

He considered this.

"I don't mean to interrupt," Bobbie Lee said, saving me further inanities, "but I have to leave."

"Of course," I said.

"Are you coming with me, Mr. Quayle? If you are, we've got to roll."

Quayle looked at me and then at gap-toothed Bobbie Lee. Poet was confused and less than satisfied with my explanations. But it was no contest. They left together.

Still, Poet's agitation was nothing to my own.

Suddenly, if the dress *was* Charlotte Vivien's I had a direct line to the woman who had picked up the missing bomb.

Did people like Charlotte Vivien lend their clothes?

At least, surely, she would know what had happened to the dress.

I went to the telephone.

But as I reached to pick it up, it rang.

The sound startled me. After the third ring I answered it. "Albert Samson."

An artificially high voice said, "Mr. Samson, it's about that meeting you wanted."

The Frog. Jesus!

I said, "What about it?"

"I can only provide two of the people concerned this

evening. The others have commitments that it will be impossible for them to break. Do you want to see the two?"

I said, "Can you arrange our meeting for tomorrow morning instead?"

After two sharp breaths she said, "I will try. I think I can."

"O.K. Eleven o'clock. But I may need to get back in touch with you later tonight, so give me your number."

"I don't really want to do that," she said. Her voice was so laden with distress that I wondered if she was in physical pain.

But I said, "Don't give me a hard time. I know where you live. If I was going to turn you in, the place would be crawling with little blue men already."

She gave me the number.

"And who do I ask for?" I said.

"You don't know my name?"

"No. But it would be easy to find out."

There was a long pause. With an unsteady voice she said, "Kathryn Morgason."

"Morgason?"

"Yes."

"As in Cab-Co Morgason?"

"Yes."

"Does he know that—"

"He hasn't got the slightest idea, Mr. Samson." And then she said, "I knew there were big risks. But when the danger is so close, it seems much more awful than I ever imagined it was going to be."

I would have asked how Sick was, but that just seemed like rubbing the risks in.

41

"MRS. VIVIEN," THE BUTLER said, "is about to go out."

In the background I heard a woman's voice ask, "Who is it, Loring?"

I said, "My name is Albert Samson. I was the detective at her murder dinner last week. And it is very important that I speak to her."

"An Albert Samson, madam," Loring said.

"Tell her it's important," I said.

But he didn't.

And then there was nothing. And it seemed to go on forever. "Hello?" I said eventually. "Is anybody out there?"

Nobody answered but neither was there a dial tone. I stayed with it.

At last an extension was lifted and another hung up. Charlotte Vivien said, "Mr. Samson?"

"Thank you for speaking to me, Mrs. Vivien."

"What is it that you want?"

"I need to see you."

"Oh yes? And what would that be about?"

"I'm working on an urgent case and a matter has come up that means I need to ask you to identify something."

"Me? Me specifically?"

"Yes. No one else will do. It is something that I am told used to be yours."

"Good heavens. What?"

"It's a dress."

"What dress?"

"I'm not good at describing clothes but I have a picture of it. I will really have to show it to you."

She paused for a long time.

I said, "Mrs. Vivien?"

She said, "As I recall, Mr. Samson, the last time we talked you wouldn't do something I asked you to. How do you have the nerve to ask a favor of me?"

"I wouldn't if it weren't *very* important. I know it sounds crazy, but it isn't. I will meet you anywhere at your convenience. If you can spare me a few minutes, just tell me where and when. I'll be there."

She sighed. "All right, Mr. Samson. A few minutes."

"Thank you."

"There is a bar on East Washington Street called McGinley's. It's a few blocks past East Street. I'll meet you there at eight-thirty."

"I'll find it."

"It has a second room, with tables."

"O.K."

She hung up.

I didn't know McGinley's but it couldn't take long to find. Eight-thirty gave me a couple of hours.

I looked around the office. Two hours. I didn't know how I should spend them. I looked at my notebook. Potential clients to call back. I looked at the telephone.

So it rang.

"Albert!" Frank said. "Hey, great, wasn't it!"

"What?"

"'What?' 'What?' Hey, everybody, he says, 'What?' Isn't this the coolest dude you'll ever meet!"

"Frank, stop pulling your wick and tell me what you're talking about."

"The commercial, of course! Everybody is raving about it."

Everybody?

"I haven't seen it," I said.

"Haven't seen it! Albert, baby!"

I choked momentarily and Frank used the time to say, "I'm at Lucy's mother's. I've got a tape. Come over. All the people from the department are on their way."

"The police department?"

Frank laughed heartily. "You are a natural, Albert, a real natural. That's what they're all saying. I won't claim that I realized it when we did the session but in the editing room it was obvious."

"What was obvious?"

"On tape you project an amateurish professionalism that is completely irresistible."

"I do?"

"Absolutely, utterly, irresistible. Lip-lickin' finger-poppin' good."

"Before you start foaming at the mouth put Lucy's mother on the phone, will you?"

"Ah, love is about sharing triumph. I can relate to that."

"Put her on the phone, Frank!"

My woman came to the telephone. I said, "Is he being committed or is he going voluntarily?"

"They're having a little party," she said. "You're the guest of honor. Are you coming?"

"What *is* this all about, kid?"

"The success of the first commercial for the Albert Samson Investigative Services Agency: ASISA."

"The what?"

"When they realized that the acronym was a palindrome it blew their minds."

"What minds?"

"Lucy did the graphics, and all the high-tech stuff sets off your aimless stuttery wholesome innocence beautifully."

"Is he contagious or something?"

"The cable company even had two calls from people saying how much they liked the commercial and asking when it would be broadcast again. Frank has booked it for two more weeks and he is considering giving up his 'filmic' ambitions to start his own ad agency."

"Somewhere in La-La Land?"

"So you haven't seen it?" she asked.

"No," I said. "I haven't seen it."

"You should."

"Oh. Right."

"I haven't felt your basic attractiveness so intensely for years."

"My what?"

"You come across well. And Frank has packaged it well. The only question is whether anybody who wants a private eye watches commercials on Cab-Co."

"I had calls from five different people while I was out."

"Albert, that's wonderful!"

"I guess so."

"What's the problem?"

"I thought it might be a joke."

"Honestly! And does that mean you haven't called any of them back?"

"Not yet."

"Well, I'll get off the phone," she said. There was a sound behind her. "Frank says, could you bring some money? He needs another eight hundred dollars."

"Don't we all."

"Sort it out with him yourself."

"Look, I don't know whether I'm going to be able to get there. I've got an appointment on the east side at eight-thirty."

"I thought you hadn't called any of those people."

"It's about another case."

"Suddenly it's nonstop business, eh?"

"Yeah," I said.

"Well," my woman said, "you could sound a little more cheerful about it."

* * *

But I didn't call any of the message-leavers.

My brain was too full.

I wandered around my rooms for a few minutes. Then went downstairs to say hello to Mom. She'd like to hear about the response to the commercial. Might mean she'd get some rent one day.

But Mom wasn't there.

Nor was there any sign of Norman.

I went back up and studied Bobbie's drawing of Wool Glove Woman and wrote up what I had done for the Animals and then did nothing very useful at all.

42

McGINLEY'S WAS EASY TO find so I was ten minutes early. It was a small building with its own parking lot. A sign on the door advised, "No shirt, no shoes, no service."

The second room was to the left past a sign on the wall that said, "This phone cuts off all calls after three minutes." It was not isolated from the main bar. It had round tables, each with six chairs. Icons from Notre Dame football teams hung on the walls.

There were no genuflections to north-side chic. McGinley's was an Irish version of the generic ordinary bar you can find anywhere in town and I'd spent many a melancholy baby hour in them, one year or another. It was an extraordinary place for Charlotte Vivien to fix a meeting in.

I took a beer to an empty table and settled. I expected to be kept waiting but Charlotte Vivien was a couple of minutes early. I didn't see her enter. When I recognized her, she was already walking toward me carrying a bottle of beer and a glass.

She wore an expensive trouser suit, and a few heads

turned as she approached my table. I rose and pulled out a chair.

"Thank you," she said.

"Thank you for meeting me."

She sat. "What's this about a dress, Mr. Samson?"

I put Bobbie's drawing before her.

She looked at it on the table. But then she picked it up. She looked at me.

"Do you recognize it?" I asked.

"The dress is very much like one that . . . that I bought before Christmas." She put the picture down.

"Do you still have it?"

She shook her head. "This is all very peculiar, Mr. Samson."

"I'm sorry about that. But I need to know."

"Well, I'm 'sorry' too, but I'm not going to answer your questions without some form of explanation, much as I like to help people who are trying to better themselves."

"I have been hired to identify and locate a woman and this drawing was made from the description a witness gave of her."

"Identify as well as locate?" she said. "I take it this is not just a missing persons case."

"That's correct."

"But is it this black woman in the drawing that you are trying to find?"

"Yes."

"Why?"

"The woman may have taken something," I said.

We sat looking at each other for a moment.

"You don't intend to tell me what she took?"

"I can't."

"And your witness didn't know who the woman was."

"No. Nor does my witness have a very good memory for faces. She does, however, remember clothes and, quite by accident, another person saw the drawing and immediately identified the dress as one of yours."

"Good gracious!" she said. "Who in the world claims to know my clothes well enough to say that a dress is mine?"

I said, "I can't tell you that either."

"Oh, honestly!" she said.

"I assure you, there is nothing sinister about the identi-fication of the dress as yours."

"I'm going to lose sleep trying to work out who it was," she said, but there wasn't much conviction about the way she said it. Maybe she led a life where lots of people followed her every frill.

"I'm sorry," I said.

"So," she said. She looked again at the picture. "There is some urgency about finding this woman?"

"There is."

"Is she . . . in danger?"

"She may be."

"From you?"

"No."

"From whom? Or what?"

"I'm afraid I can't—"

"You can't tell me much, can you, Mr. Samson? But you damn well expect me to tell you any little thing you want to know."

"It *is* important, Mrs. Vivien. That's why I've made such an effort to see you this evening."

Charlotte Vivien said, "It's a nice drawing, but I am not all that sure that this dress is the one I used to have."

"Used to have?"

"That's right. I no longer own the garment your anony-mous source remembers."

"Where is it?"

"Where is it?" she mimicked. "How about 'Where is it, please?'"

"This is not a game, Mrs. Vivien. But if you would be so kind and gracious, I would be grateful to know where the dress in question might be found now, please."

"I'm sorry. I'm sorry." She set her glass aside and took a long pull from the bottle of beer. "One way and another life has been very complicated for me lately. In moments of enthusiasm I put myself forward as a certain sort of person and then the enthusiasm fades and I find myself trapped by

the façade I've created and I long to be free. So I make some
contrary decisions and they lead to involvements that make
me shudder when I wake up in the morning and think about
them."

I had been involved in one of her enthusiasms and had
shuddered myself. But that wasn't what Charlotte Vivien was
talking about. What, though? A stranger's head on the pillow?

I said, "Being in charge of one's own destiny is both the
greatest up and the greatest down of being alive."

"Yes," she said. She looked at me. "Who said that?"

"I did."

"Oh. Well." She studied the beer bottle and then flicked
at it half a dozen times with the nail of her index finger.
"When I feel things slipping out of control I get irritable. I
don't know, Mr. Samson. What am I going to do?"

"About what?"

"About . . ." She looked up at me again. With a short
rush of breath she said something like, "Ha." Then, "But you
don't want to know about my troubles."

"I am happy to hear about your troubles. They'll make a
change from my own."

But her confessional moment had passed and she tuned
me back to my proper place in her universe. She said, "What
were we talking about?"

"I was trying to find out what happened to the dress."

"I don't keep clothes that I have no more use for."

"So you do what, throw them away?"

"No, no. Most go to a Next to New charity store, though
I do sometimes give things to the people who work for me."

She knew full well what I was going to ask next, but she
waited for me anyway. "And do you remember what you did
with this particular dress?"

She thought. "Probably the Next to New. But you know
how things are. Sometimes you have a clear visual picture of
something you've done and sometimes you don't. I don't
really remember."

"Do you know how long ago you got rid of it?"

"I certainly remember the last time I wore it."

"Which was?"

"To a party in January. *That* I remember extremely clearly, because the man I was with spilled wine over me and then made it far worse by trying to wipe it off."

"And would you have given the dress away soon after that?"

"I would think so. But I don't remember. Sorry."

"If it was to a person, who might it have been?"

For some reason she reacted slightly when I asked her this. But after a moment she said, "Well, I have a house-keeper and I sometimes give her things."

"Do I take it that she is not likely to be the person in the drawing?"

"Ayesha? No, no. She's the right color but the wrong side of sixty, and dumpy."

"So any clothes you give her are for somebody else anyway."

"Yes."

"Do you know who?"

"What do you mean?"

"Do you know who Ayesha passes clothes on to?"

"Not really."

"Is there anybody else you give clothes to?"

"I must have given things of one kind or another to all my staff."

"How many of those are there?"

"You've met Loring. I also have a handyman, David."

"Would you give dresses to them?"

"I don't remember ever giving them dresses. Though some of my friends seem to think Loring might well have an inclination toward that kind of thing."

"You wouldn't give dresses to friends?"

"No, no."

"To your children?"

"Sheree wouldn't be seen dead in a dress like this. And my son's girlfriend is absolutely minute and only seems to wear denim with carefully picked holes in it."

"Mrs. Vivien, if I don't have any luck at the Next to New, may I show the drawing to your employees?"

"If you must," she said.

"Where is the charity store?"

She gave me the address.

"And do your employees work for you every day?"

"Loring lives in. The others come each day, yes."

"O.K. I'll check the Next to New tomorrow."

She sat back. "Is that it?"

"That's it, Mrs. Vivien. Thank you very much indeed."

"May I ask you a favor now?"

"Sure."

"Let me know what you find out about the dress."

"If I can, I will."

She shook her head. "You won't even promise me that after all the questions I've answered." She shook her head.

I said, "Mrs. Vivien, may I ask you a completely irrelevant question?"

She didn't answer at once. Then she said, "No, I don't think you may. I don't much like conversations that are one-way traffic" She got up and left without another word.

I watched her go.

What I wanted to ask was how she knew the bar.

She passed from my sight and I was about to gather up the drawing when I noticed a figure leave a barstool and head for the door.

The figure was female, though dressed in unisex jeans and a ski jacket. The figure turned toward me and winked and then passed out of sight in the same direction as Charlotte Vivien.

The figure was Bobbie Lee Leonard.

BEFORE I LEFT McGINLEY'S, I called my woman. Her daughter, Lucy, answered the phone. "Albert, where are you!" she said. "We've been waiting!"

"Get your mother, please. I only have three minutes."

"What?"

"Your mother. I need to speak to her."

"O.K. O.K. But get your ass over here, hear?"

"Lucy . . ." I began again, with impatience. But she was gone.

It seemed forever before my woman took her place. But it was only about thirty seconds. And counting. She said, "I know you Hollywood types go in for late arrivals and grand entrances but I think you'd better hurry. Your fan club is running out of patience."

"Ho-ho."

"Are you coming over, Al?"

"Only after they've left. How long should I leave it?"

"An hour should do it. They'll have finished the beer by then and they've already gotten tired of patting each other on the back."

"I'll go home first, then, and pick up a six-pack on the way. It's not Sunday, is it?"

"No, it's not Sunday. What's the matter, TV star? The flunky who counts days for you gone to the john?"

I stopped at the Liquor Locker across from the office and then locked the liquor in my trunk before ascending my stairs.

I should have been more alert. I would have heard the car door slam.

What I did hear was footsteps at the bottom of the stairs as I put the key in my door. I looked down. Someone in a cape and broad-brimmed hat was outlined in the streetlight. The someone was making its way up the stairs. There was an unsteadiness of step about the someone's progress.

It was not anyone I recognized and as it got closer I saw that my visitor was a woman. Hopes that her trek up the stairs was a mistake vanished four steps below me when she said, "Mr. Samson? Mr. Samson?"

I thought about denying myself, but, typically, I didn't act fast enough.

She said. "I *knew* you had to be out. I just knew it!"

I said. "Uh."

She arrived on the landing. I saw that she wore extremely high heels and that was enough to account for the wobbles up the stairs.

"Excuse me," I said. "Do I know you?"

"No, no," she said. "Can we go in?"

"What?"

"In. Can we go in now? It's not very comfortable out here, is it? And I have been waiting for you. It's only been twenty minutes, but I was ready to stay all night if I had to. See, I knew you were out. It was the only humane explanation and if there's one thing that I know about you it is that you are humane."

I said, "I don't mean to be inhospitable, but what is it that you want?"

"I left messages when I called. But you haven't gotten them, because you've been out! Of course I didn't explain anything on the phone. I find I can't bare my soul to an answering machine. But I did call three times."

Ah.

"Ah," I said.

"Please. Can we go in?"

We went in.

"It's just like I thought it would be," she said immediately.

I pointed to my Client's Chair. "Have a seat," I said. "Miss . . . ?"

"Seals," she said. "Monique Seals. Of course Monique isn't the name my parents gave me."

"Of course," I said.

I looked at my watch. I looked at Monique Seals. I sat down. I said, "Now, what was it that you wanted me to look into for you, Miss Seals?"

"It's Mrs. Ashworth."

"Excuse me?"

"I'm married. My married name is Ashworth, but Monique Seals is how I think of myself."

"I see."

"No, you don't," she said, "but *I* see, very clearly." She leaned forward.

"Excuse me?"

"What I am about to say is going to embarrass you," she said.

"Then please don't say it."

"No, honestly. It will!"

"Miss Seals. Mrs. Ashworth. I think—"

"I saw you on television," she said. "And I knew, just knew, that you were *different.*"

"Different from what, ma'am?"

"I could tell it by the eyes. And by the way you moved your little head when you seemed uncomfortable. You're not like other men, are you?"

"Uh, I'm not sure I exactly—"

"And so attractive! But you must get tired of women telling you that, I bet." She grinned at me.

I couldn't think of anything to say.

"How old do you think I am?"

"Excuse me?"

"How old do I look? Take a guess. Don't be shy."

"I couldn't begin . . ."

"Thirty-nine years old. But I don't look more than twenty-eight or twenty-nine, do I? Do I?"

"Uh . . ."

"No, I know I don't. That's because I take care of myself, always have. Even when I was itty-bitty I stayed out of the sun and ate all my vegetables. I have an instinct for things like that."

"Look . . ."

"And so when I had an instinct about you, I just knew I was right! You see, I saw you on TV. So human and frail and yet so overpoweringly capable and come-hither. And I knew that if anybody could help me, you could. And you can. I know you can, can't you? Why so silent?"

"I'm afraid," I said, "that at the moment my caseload is very heavy, Miss Seals. I don't know exactly what it is that you would have liked me to do for you, but—"

She stood up abruptly. The friendliness on her face flipped to hostility. "You're not going to, are you? You won't help me. You won't even try!"

I stood up and began to move toward the door. The idea was to open it for her.

But as I moved around the desk, she stretched out one hand to restrain me by the arm. "Don't!" she said. With the other hand she opened her cape.

From the waistband of dark blue slacks she pulled out a gun.

I stopped where I was.

"Don't do anything foolish now," she said.

"I . . . I . . ."

She beamed. "Surprised you, huh?"

I nodded.

"You bastards are all alike," she said.

"Miss Seals," I began.

"Mrs. Ashworth," she said.

"Mrs. Ashworth—"

"I told you!" she shouted. "I think of myself as Monique Seals."

I lunged for the gun.

I READ ONCE THAT PEOPLE trained in close-quarter
combat laugh at cowboy and copboy movies where people
stick .45s in each other's backs or ribs. The point is that if the
gun is that close, a sudden move with an arm will knock the
weapon's aim away more quickly than the weapon-bearer can
pull the trigger. Of course trained people also know what to
do next. Twist, grunt, lever. Bad guy on the floor cringing for
mercy; good guy shoving the barrel up the bad guy's nostril
and saying. "Make my quota."

And then, because the bad guy's read the book too, he
makes a quick move with *his* arm, because up the nostril is
close, like the back or ribs.

Me, I just went by instinct.

I pushed the gun away with one hand and grabbed at
Seals-Ashworth's wrist with the other.

She didn't resist. I got the gun out of her hand and
pushed her away. She dropped to the floor in a heap.

I stood over her and my body caught up with what I had
done. I began to pant, to feel faint.

I edged back and sat on my desk.

We stayed like that in silence—apart from heavy breathing—for a long time.

When I got my breath I called the police.

The first patrolman arrived about ten minutes later. He pounded on the door.

I carried the gun by the barrel and opened the door for him.

He was about six feet six and twenty years old and he said, "I got a call there was an incident with a firearm here but that it's over. That right, mister?"

"Yes," I said. I held the pistol up for him to see. "The woman on the floor pulled this on me. I took it away from her."

"Hey, buddy," he said. "We don't like to get involved in domestic disputes where people end up dropping charges."

"This is not a domestic dispute," I said. "I've never met this woman before tonight."

"Yeah, yeah. Until you decide to kiss and make up."

Then Miss-Mrs. Seals-Ashworth said, "He tried to rape me."

"What?" the patrolman said.

"What?" I said.

"I came here to hire him and he pulled that gun he's holding and he tried to rape rape rape me." She began to cry.

The young cop turned my way. He frowned. "That's a serious charge, fella." His hand went to his holster. "You better give that gun to me."

"My pleasure," I said. I held it out. He took it by the barrel. Then he wasn't quite sure what to do with it.

"He tried to rape me," Seals-Ashworth said again.

"What you got to say about that, buddy?"

"I say it's a load of bull," I said. I felt tired.

"No it isn't!" Seals-Ashworth said.

The officer looked at her and then looked at me.

I said, "*I* was the one who called the police."

"It was to cover what you did," she said.

"I'm afraid the poor woman is not very well," I said.

Seals-Ashworth did some more tears. "And I said you were humane!" she said. "How young and innocent can I be?"

The young and innocent patrolman turned back and forth between us.

Then we all heard footsteps running up my outside stairs. We looked at the door and a second police officer, a sergeant, jumped into the room.

"Wise, what the hell are you doing coming into the scene of a gun incident before your goddamn backup has arrived?"

The tall young patrolman said, "Dispatch said the caller said it was over."

"So you walk up to the front door like a bit of target practice before you *know*."

"But it is over, Sarge. Only I can't figure out what happened."

The sergeant looked at me. Then he looked at Seals-Ashworth on the floor. "Oh fuck," he said. "I take it all back."

The patrolman said, "What?"

The sergeant said, "Hello, Cola."

Seals-Ashworth sat up and said, "Hello, Jack."

Jack turned to me and said, "You must have been on TV for something recently, right?"

"Uh, right," I said.

"So Cola pulled a gun on you, right."

"Yeah."

"What did she make you do? Stand on your head? Take your shoes off?" He turned to her. "What was it this time, Cola?"

"Nothin'," she said.

"I took the gun off her."

"Ooo, big tough guy," Sergeant Jack said.

The young patrolman was still holding the gun gingerly by its barrel.

Jack said, "That it?"

"Yeah."

"Give it to me," Jack said. The patrolman gave it to him.

Jack glanced at the gun and then pointed it between my eyes.

"Hey, come on!" I said.

He pulled the trigger.

I twisted to the side, but I was miles too late.

However, there was no explosion. No sudden death. No meeting with St. Peter to present my lame excuses.

All that happened was that I cricked my neck.

Jack said, "Replica. If you don't know anything about guns, they're pretty frightening. We must have taken six or eight or ten of these things off her in the last two years alone. I don't know where the hell she gets them."

"I got my sources," Cola Seals-Ashworth said.

"Price of fame," Jack said.

45

"THE PRICE OF SEX APPEAL," my woman said.

"It was not funny," I said.

"No, I suppose it wasn't." She laughed.

I moved to the other end of the couch. I said, "Come on! I was on TV once a few years ago and nobody noticed."

"I can't help that. This time you radiated that special pheromone. Even I felt it. I reacted to it. And if anybody should know better . . ."

"Thanks."

She laughed again.

"Look, kid, I've got problems," I said.

"Whether to hire a social secretary?"

I said nothing. That's how she knew I had something serious to talk about.

She said, "Is it about that picture?"

Bobbie Lee's drawing. "Partly," I said.

She waited.

"I'm in an extremely difficult position. I don't know what to do. Whether I should go to the cops, or what."

My woman and I don't talk about details of work.

Because I was breaking the rule with intent, she knew it was important.

"Come on," she said. We retreated to her bedroom where we wouldn't be interrupted.

She listened as I explained how I had come to be involved with the most wanted criminal organization in Indianapolis.

"You? With the Scum Front?" She couldn't help herself.

"Me."

"But why did they come to *you?*"

"They said it was because I work alone."

My woman frowned. "How did they know that?"

"I don't know. Maybe my ads in the paper. But they tried me out before they revealed who they were."

I described Kate King's first visits and how they had led to visits by the Animals and how I'd been told that if I didn't look for the missing bomb, nobody would.

"Well . . ." my woman said. Code for "I sort of see why you did it, but I think you're nuts to have gotten involved."

I told her how I'd tried to protect myself by insisting that they leave no more bombs anywhere while I was on the case.

"That's something, I suppose."

Then I told her what I'd done and how I'd found Cecil Redman and how that information had led me to the Frog.

"You know who one of them is! You're sure?"

And I explained about Dancing Girl and her description of the woman who had followed the Frog.

"And that's what this is about?" she said, pointing at the drawing.

"Yep. That's almost certainly the person who picked up the bomb."

"Hmmmm."

I told her about the chance identification of the dress in the picture. And I began to talk about my bar meeting with Charlotte Vivien.

"Hang on, hang on," my woman said.

"What?"

"Let me see that picture again."

I held it up for her.

She looked at it for a moment. Then at me.

"What's wrong?" I asked.

"You saw this and you're trying to identify the dress?"

"Yeah."

"You're a jerk," she said.

"What do you mean?"

"You are doing exactly what your dancing witness did. You're only looking at the clothes. I know it's nicely drawn and all that, but what's the interest?"

"Well, it's the only thing I have a detailed description of."

"So what?"

I shook my head.

"You're a nice man, Albert. Open, accepting of people and unusual because of that. But you forget where you live sometimes."

"I don't understand what you're saying."

My woman said, "Get back to basics, gumshoe. What is it that you really have here?"

"Tell me."

"You have a witness who saw the woman in the picture follow your Frog when she was planting a bomb."

"Right."

"And people don't just follow other people for the hell of it, so you deduce that the odds are good that the woman in the picture picked the bomb up."

"Yeah."

"But how did the woman in the picture know your Frog was worth following?"

"I don't know yet. I need to identify her first."

"And you're trying to do that through the clothes she wore."

"The clothes are supposed to be unique."

"But Al! Your Frog turns out to be a well-off suburban Indianapolis housewife!"

"Yeah."

"Come on, man! You live in the northernmost southern city of America. Forget the damn dress. Forget Charlotte

Vivien. How many *black* women does your white Indianapolis Scum Front housewife know? And how many of those
black women could conceivably know enough about your
Frog to work out that she plants bombs? Your Frog's the one
who can tell you who this woman is. Talk to her!"

46

OF COURSE, THAT WAS MORE or less what I had planned
to do at my Front meeting in the morning. I just hadn't quite
gotten the situation in focus.

"You're tired," my woman said.

"Yeah."

"Too much is happening too quickly for you."

"Yeah. And you're right about something else too," I said.

"What's that?"

"I'm a jerk."

But it was too late to call Mrs. Morgason/the Frog without
blowing the whole thing wide open in her household. First
thing in the morning would have to do. But no way would I
wait for the eleven o'clock meeting.

However, I was not good company during the night. By
two-thirty A.M. we decided that I should go home if I wasn't
going to be able to sleep without tossing, turning and
disarming intruders.

Social workers need their z's.

Naturally, once I was in my car I wasn't sleepy at all.

I drove to 23rd Street. There was a chance that the Rubble Belt Think Tank would be working late and the HQ would show a light.

But the place was dark and quiet.

Elsewhere in the city there were sirens calling in the darkness, but their charms did not work on me.

There was nothing to do but go home. There, eventually, I slept.

The telephone woke me at ten past eight. It was the police. A woman's voice.

It didn't make sense to me.

"You want what?" I said.

"I said, I need to take your statement this morning."

"Who did you say you were?"

"Sergeant Ivory Prisco."

"Do I know you?"

"No, sir, I don't think so."

"Well, what kind of statement are you talking about? My philosophy of life, or what?"

"Please don't be facetious, Mr. Samson. I'm only doing my job."

"Please continue doing it to the extent of telling me what you're talking about."

"Just how many involvements with the police have you had in the last twelve hours?"

"Twelve hours? That seems like a lifetime."

"Does the name Cola Lowis mean anything to you?"

"Nothing whatever."

"Welsey Avenue?"

"Nothing."

"But I understand that she threatened you with a replica revolver last night."

"Ah," I said.

"Am I beginning to get through to you, Mr. Samson?"

"You are, Sergeant Prisco."

"We've decided to try to have Ms Lowis committed for

treatment, but to do that we need a formal statement describing exactly what she did to you."

"I see. And if all she did was make a god-awful nuisance of herself?"

"I need the details. Can we fix a time for me to come by this morning?"

I hesitated.

"Mr. Samson?"

"Will it take long?"

"No sir, I wouldn't think so."

"Well, how about nine o'clock, Sergeant Prisco? My office is only five minutes from your office."

"That'll be fine," Ivory Prisco said.

Nine o'clock. Done by nine-fifteen. I could be with the Frog on 91st Street by quarter to ten.

I called her.

Nobody answered. O.K. So Sick wasn't so sick today. And was being taken to school? Try again in a few minutes.

I put coffee on and did some abluting.

I called the Frog again at eight-thirty. And at twenty to nine.

I was getting dressed when I heard the doorbell. The time was eight forty-five.

But it was not Sergeant Prisco. There was nobody there when I opened the door. But "nobody" had left me an envelope.

Before I picked it up I stepped out to the edge of the porch to look up and down the street. But I saw nothing that attracted my attention.

I brought the envelope inside and opened it. And pulled out a sheet of paper stuck with words and letters cut from newspapers.

The message read: "Our missing package was recovered last night. Your services are no longer required. Do NOT contact any of us or reveal ANY information to police or you put what you value at GREAT risk. Repeat: GREAT risk. Keep all money. Forget us."

So there it was. Fired.

And threatened.

I went outside and studied the street again. Pointlessly.

I came back in and reread the note.

It made me angry.

I sat down and dialed the Frog's number and let it ring thirty times and only gave it up when the doorbell rang.

SERGEANT PRISCO APOLOGIZED for being a few minutes early. "It's not as much trouble to park round here as it is downtown," she said by way of explanation.

I didn't know what to say. "Would you like some coffee?"

"Great. Thanks. Black. No sugar."

That gave me a couple of minutes to get my head together.

I brought back two mugs. She sat in my Client's Chair. I retreated to my own.

I fondled my mug like it was a precious thing. I felt bleary, stupid and tired. Anger was giving way to confusion. It didn't help at all that confusion was becoming a way of life.

"I don't feel very bright," I said.

"It must have been a disturbing experience," she said.

"What? Oh. Yeah, a bit."

"I'll be gentle," she said.

"What?"

She waited.

"Oh," I said. "A joke. Huh."

She took a sheet of paper from a zippered case. "I have

the report from the officers who attended the incident last night. It seems clear enough, but maybe if I read it to you . . ."

The written material the police had provided was accurate, if brief. It reminded me of what had happened and I added more detail about Cola Lowis/Monique Seals/Mrs. Ashworth's words before she had pulled the replica gun. But we did not make a lengthy job of it.

After I signed the statement form I said, "I understand that Ms Lowis has done this kind of thing before."

"Yeah, but we've had trouble getting statements from victims because they don't like to admit how foolish they looked."

"It was all over pretty quickly," I said.

"Course you might have waited a lot longer for officers to respond to your call if it had happened a couple of hours later."

"I don't understand," I said.

"Don't you watch the TV in the morning?"

"Not usually."

"So you haven't heard?"

"Heard what?"

Ivory Prisco leaned forward. "Those goddamn Scum Fronters went and did it."

"What?"

"They set one off. A bomb."

My heart jumped yet again from jog to full sprint.

"They blew up a government office building on Ohio Street."

"Last night?"

"A little before two. There's a night watchman in intensive care."

I was losing the power of speech.

"People who put bombs around like that just aren't *normal,* you know?" Ivory Prisco said. "Sure as can be, they were always going to blow something up and I'll tell you this," Ivory Prisco said. "The whole damn city's going to be after those bastards now."

AS SOON AS IVORY PRISCO left I called the police
department. Miller was at his desk. He said, "I don't have any
spare time, Al. I nearly didn't take the call."

My voice shook. "You've got time for this, Jerry."

Miller paused. Then he said, "What's that?"

"I can tell you things about the Scum Front. I've done
things for them."

"What?"

"You heard."

"What can you tell me? What have you done?"

"I think I better come down."

It felt like I could hear him thinking. The he said, "O.K.
Now."

"I'll be on my way in five minutes," I said.

I hung up. I was breathing hard.

I stood and tried to remember where all the Scum Front
bits and pieces were. But I felt faint. I sat down.

The telephone rang.

I considered not answering it.

I went halfway. I picked up the receiver but said nothing.

"Al? Albert?"

My woman.

I said, "Have you heard?"

"Heard what?"

"The bastards blew a building up. On Ohio Street. I used to *live* in a building on Ohio Street."

"The radio news said there was an explosion downtown."

"They left me a letter this morning. They fired me. They threatened me. And all the time they'd already gone and blown up a building."

"The Scum Front did that?"

I hesitated. "A cop told me they did."

"The reporter on the radio said it might be somebody else. They sent a message, but it was about abortion."

"What!?"

"'According to reports from senior police officials,' was what the radio said."

I tried to speak, but it came out as unintelligible sound.

"Besides, Al," my woman said, "you know who one of them is. If they were going to start blowing things up wouldn't they, like, kill you first or something?"

"I didn't think."

"That's what women are for," she said. It was a comment meant to lead to lighter subjects.

"I've just made the most colossal mistake," I said.

"What's the problem?"

"I told Jerry Miller."

There was a long silence at the other end of the phone.

"I told him I know things about the Scum Front."

"Oh, Al," my woman said.

HOW STUPID IS IT POSSIBLE to be?

The people with the missing bomb blew up the building on Ohio Street. The Scummies had only "recovered" it because it had been set off by whoever had taken it.

A mistake in logic of the most elementary kind.

How could I do that? About something so important?

Because a cop had told me, and I took it at face value.

A cop!

And because I was stressed out.

And because my life was being changed all around me. Murder dinner parties and commercials and too many clients.

Because I was being hurried about everything.

Because it was all too much.

And because I was plain and simple fucking-A, world-class, mega-death stupid, stupid, stupid, stupid, stupid, stupid.

50

I TOOK MY TIME.

I tried to plan what I would say.

It wasn't easy. I didn't want to say anything. But if I didn't go to Miller, he would come to me.

He might not come in his own body but, oh yes, he would come. In a hundred other bodies, each one dressed in blue and carrying a gun.

When troubles come, they come not single spies but in battalion.

When detective panics, he thinks not of now but of lines force-memorized as a child.

I walked slowly around my rooms. I sought inspiration.

All I could think of was some form of complete denial. "Oh, just my little joke, Jerry. Sorry if you didn't think it was funny."

That would go down a bomb.

Because I feared he would order a search of my office, I collected all the physical evidence connecting me to the Scum Front. Today's paste-up message and the tape recording I'd made of them were the most damning. I put them in an envelope. I added the hanky.

On the envelope I wrote, "Keep secure. Hand over only to Albert Samson or his heirs." I signed it. I sealed it with cellophane tape.

Then I put that envelope in a bigger one.

I found some stamps.

And my lawyer's address.

And I left the zip code off. The mail people punish you for that. They take an extra day to deliver. Or maybe a week.

The phone rang before I left.

I didn't answer it, but after the noise stopped, I switched my answering machine on.

Miller left word downstairs that I should be passed straight through when I arrived.

I knew the way. I had been to his office often enough. All his offices. Even to his desk, when he first got promoted to detective and was too green and too unimportant to have enclosed space on his own.

We went back a long way together, did Miller and I. High school kids who didn't grow into the groups we were expected to measure ourselves by. Kids who gravitated toward each other, though black and white didn't mix then even as much as they do now here in the city nicknamed Naptown. Miller and I were two misfits who talked in monosyllables and who, together, took some cars on brief, truly joyful excursions.

Until we'd taken a turn too fast. I was at the wheel, but it could have been either of us.

We walked away.

But we learned that we cared whether we lived or died.

That certain knowledge further distanced us from the groups—they're organized into gangs these days—that we were expected to hang out with.

It also led each of us toward the power of words. Reminiscing about joyrides is at first safer but eventually better than the real thing.

Yes, I'd known Miller for a long time.

* * *

It wasn't the legs that gave out. It was the belly. When I got off the elevator, I turned and ran for the john.

I got through the door, but not as far as a sink.

I threw up first on the run. Then standing still, then kneeling.

Everything in my life was coming back to me. The pressure. My ambitions. It was all lying on the tiles.

I shook. I turned cold.

A man with scuffed brown shoes and green checked socks and no cuffs stood somewhere near.

He said, "There's a mop in the closet by the paper towels."

I tried to say, "Thanks."

He said, "Amazing! No carrot!"

Then he left.

And, as I kneeled, my head began to clear.

Miller was not just a cop who stood between me and my freedom. He was a guy whose hopes and dreams I knew as well as I knew my own.

Yes. Yes.

I stood. I cleaned myself and my mess as best as I could.

And then I went to see my buddy.

MILLER STOOD AT HIS DOOR, waiting. He didn't smile. He didn't offer a hand. He was Captain Miller.

He closed the door behind us.

"Trouble parking?" he said.

"Yeah, but that's not why I'm late."

He looked at my shirt. "Why are you late?"

"Because I've made the most awful mistake."

He did not speak or move.

I said, "Do you have a tape recorder going here?"

"No. Do you want one?"

"No, I don't want one. And I don't know whether to believe you."

"I wouldn't lie to you."

"Yes you would."

He smiled slightly. He opened a desk drawer.

I looked.

A tape recorder was running. The handwritten label on the cassette read, "Albert Samson: Scum Front," and gave the date.

"Kill it," I said.

He turned the machine off.

"The tape," I said. I put out a hand.

"Why?"

"In case it's voice-activated."

"Ah."

He took the tape from the machine and passed it to me.

"You swear on your mother's Bible and Wendy's wedge that there's no other recording of any kind going on here?"

"I swear. You didn't give me time to set up anything cute. And besides," he said, "you're a friend. Why should I need more than one?"

I pulled a chair over to the window behind his desk. I sat and put my feet up on the sill.

Miller turned his own chair and we shared the view of the Market Square Arena parking lot.

"I thought about trying to bullshit you," I said.

"Oh yeah?" He waited.

"They came to me, Jerry. I was just sitting at home, minding my own business, and they came to me."

"Why?"

"Because of the bomb they left in the Merchants Bank Building."

"The one that wasn't there?"

"Somebody took it. They wanted me to get it back."

"Why you, Al?"

My woman had asked the same question. I repeated what I had been told, "Because I work alone."

Miller said, "So what happened?"

"They said if I didn't look for their bomb, then nobody would."

"Oh yeah?"

"They said I was the only chance of keeping whoever took it from using it and maybe killing somebody." I turned to him. "I hear there was a guy hurt in the explosion."

"Yeah. They don't think he'll die, though."

"Well, that's something."

"So why didn't you come to me?" he said.

"They were very edgy. They were looking for any sign that I was going to the cops. They followed me around and threatened me. They've got a lot to lose if they're caught and they needed to convince themselves they could trust me. I don't know. Yes, I could have come to you and set them up. But finding the missing bomb seemed more important. So I didn't. Instead I made them promise they wouldn't leave any new bombs while I was on the case."

"And?"

"I got a message this morning saying they had 'recovered' their 'missing package' and no longer required my services. I thought they'd found it and set it off."

We sat, quiet, for a moment. I knew what he was going to ask. I said, "I can't tell you who they are. Not yet."

"I don't believe this," he said.

"I'm sorry."

"You're protecting them? Terrorists? Do you know what's going to happen to you?"

"They didn't blow the building up. The people who took the missing bomb—"

"How the hell do you know that?" He shouted at me, though he was speaking barely louder than a whisper.

I said, "I know these people now. I don't believe they did it."

"And who did?"

"I don't know."

"You been working on it . . . how long?"

"A few days."

"Do you have any leads?"

"I have a lead."

"And are you going to tell me about *that*?"

"No. I give it to you and it goes out of control."

He shook his head. "I don't understand," he said.

"What don't you understand?"

He swiveled to face me. "Do you seriously expect me to let you walk out of here?"

"I think you should," I said.

"Why's that?"

"Because if you don't, my lead will evaporate and you won't have any idea how to get to the people who set off the bomb."

"Because you won't tell us what you know?"

"I won't tell you anything."

"Even though you'll spend the rest of your life in jail."

I shrugged.

"Jesus God!" he said. He shook his head. "What kind of world do you think you live in, Al? Don't you have any idea what you're playing with here? You'll be *lucky* if all that happens is that you go to jail and they take your license. Terrorism carries the death penalty in this state, you know."

"Am *I* a terrorist now?"

"If they don't get somebody else they can prosecute."

"Well, all I know is that I have a good lead on the person who picked up the bomb from the Merchants Bank Building."

"It's a *good* lead now? A minute ago it was just a lead."

"I believe I know someone who can virtually identify the person who took the bomb."

"Virtually identify? What does 'virtually identify' mean in English? Does it bear *any* relationship to what I understand by the concept of identification?"

"It should."

"And I'm supposed to let you walk out of here?"

"I think that's your best bet."

"And I am supposed to carry the can if you come up empty?"

"Jerry," I said. "did you tell anybody that I was coming in?"

"Of course I did," he said.

"Your secretary maybe. But did you tell anybody why? What I said on the phone?"

He sighed. "No."

"Why not?"

"I didn't think you'd find the atmosphere of fourteen guys with the devil in their eyes and their guns up your nose conducive to constructive communicative intercourse."

"And you also didn't think—after all the help you've given me over the years—that you should share a chance to crack the biggest case of the decade."

He said nothing.

"You haven't run out of ambitions, have you? You think you might make a pretty damned good Chief of Police, if anybody ever decided to give a black guy a shot at it. Don't you?"

"I'm what you might call a dark horse," he said.

I laughed.

"What you laughing at, man?"

"I'm laughing because until just then I wasn't *absolutely* sure you didn't have another tape recorder running."

He laughed too.

We both laughed.

And then I put my feet back on the floor and walked out.

52

IT WAS LIKE BEING BORN again. My brain and body were free. In the elevator I wanted to skip down the stairs. I wanted to sing.

How the woman with the tag that read "Lt. Sheryl Turk" would have taken an unrehearsed rendition of "The First Day of the Rest of My Life," I didn't know.

But I couldn't keep from saying something. The idea of a song reminded me. I said, "You know, there's an Indy singer named Pat Webb who thinks Lawrence Township ought to be renamed 'Larry.'"

She looked at me.

"To make it more casual and friendly and inviting."

"Do I know you?" she asked. But the doors opened and I made my escape.

There are public telephones in the entrance foyer at the police department. I used one to try the Frog's number again.

No answer.

When I retrieved my quarter I remembered a cop Miller

told me about once. This guy opens all the phone change-return trays every morning and scoops them for unclaimed coins. At least he did until a buddy filled one with ketchup.

I stood shaking mind-ketchup off my hand.

I laughed aloud.

I wondered what I should do next.

What I did was go outside, turn left and cross the street to City Market.

On the mezzanine I sat with a doughnut and a cup of coffee. I drank the coffee but talked to the doughnut.

I explained my options and feelings to it. It did not object when I emphasized the need to find the Frog/Mrs. Morgason.

I have this picture, see, doughnut. The woman in it worked out that Mrs. Morgason was a bomber. So I need Mrs. Morgason to tell me about all the black women she knows.

The doughnut was not apparently impressed.

Doughnut, do you think her husband might help? Either with where she is, or with who her friends are?

Just about possible, we supposed, but the doughnut was not enthusiastic.

That led me to consider other ways to get the information. Given that Mrs. Morgason was not immediately available.

And hey, doughnut, there's already one black woman who knows Mrs. Morgason. Cecil Redman's wife's mother, who does cleaning. And hey, didn't Redman say his wife filled in sometimes when her mother got sick? And Redman's wife would be more or less the right age for the woman in the picture.

Hmmm, doughnut, maybe you've got something there.

And Cecil Redman would have told his wife that he'd seen Mrs. Morgason carrying suitcases in the rubble belt.

Could that have been clue enough for her to suspect Mrs. Morgason was a Scummie?

I sat up straight. My knees hit the table and jiggled it. The doughnut seemed to nod.

I didn't know anything about Mrs. Redman, bar a reputation for brass balls. But it beat hell out of dialing 91st Street and getting no answer.

I thanked the doughnut.

Then I ate it.

I considered explaining that life's like that, but there's only so much a doughnut can handle at any one time.

53

I GOT CAB-CO'S GENERAL number from the book.

A mellifluous voice said, "Cab-Co," and I asked to speak to Mr. Morgason.

However, the voice said, "Sorry. Mr. Morgason is not here just now. Can I have him call you?"

"When is he expected back?"

"We got the Chief of Police coming for a meeting in about an hour, but you could try after lunch."

"I need to speak with him before that, if possible. It's about his wife."

"Oh, are you a friend?"

The way she asked included a request that I say yes.

"Yes."

"Do you know where she is? Poor Mr. Morgason's been looking for her all morning."

"So he doesn't know?"

"No sir. She wasn't there when he got up. She didn't leave a message or nothing. And it's inconvenienced him something awful. But I know he's also thinking that maybe Mrs. Morgason's been kidnapped."

"Good heavens."

"It's just everybody thinks he's so rich. People who've known him all his life know better—he's being backed financially, see—but it's because he's exploded into the cable business like he has."

"But the idea of kidnap, is it a guess? Or is there something specific to suggest it?"

"He just doesn't have any idea at all where she is and that's the long and short of it. I told him, I said, Mr. Morgason, you should hire that cute detective who was on the commercial, but he didn't like that idea much."

"He didn't?"

"He said he thought the guy was just a clown trying to capitalize on his sex appeal and he probably didn't know one end of a private dick from another. He talks like that, Mr. Morgason. He doesn't mean anything by it. You got to take him the way he is."

Cecil Redman's truck wasn't parked outside the HQ, so I went over to his house on College. The pickup was in the alley at the back.

I had to knock several times but eventually Redman himself answered the door. He squinted sleepily and said, "You the guy came looking for me."

"That's right."

"What you want now?"

"I need to talk to your wife."

He shook his head to clear his mind. He wasn't immediately successful. He rubbed a cheek. "You what?"

"Your wife."

"Louanne?" he said. He looked back into the hall of the house. He stepped onto the stoop and pulled the door shut behind him.

I said, "Do you know where she lives? Or works?"

"What you hassle me about stuff like that for?"

"You said you went to 91st Street to ask her mother where Louanne lives now."

"I gave Momma a lift home. And that's where Louanne

be, home with her momma." His tone was sneering, but I passed the opportunity to comment that a lot of fine, mature people live with their parents these days.

I said, "O.K. So where does her mother live?"

"I tell you where she *used* to live. She used to live under the goddamn lions."

"What?"

"Her house where the lions in the zoo be now, man."

"Oh, I see."

"Anyhow, this time of day you going to find her at work. Every day for more than thirty years, except she's sick. Proud as hell of that. Stayed with the same family through three houses, only now she got to go to goddamn 91st Street. Don't make no sense to me."

"I've called up there. Nobody answers the phone."

He shrugged.

"What time does she start work?"

"I don't know, man. But she go early. Come back early too."

"Does she answer the phone?"

"I never called her."

"And do you know where she lives now?"

"Yeah, she got a little house. West 14th Street, across the river. A brown house, on a corner."

He explained how to get to it.

"And what's her name?" I asked.

"Effie. Effie Hawk, man."

"Hawkman?"

"No no. Just goddamn Hawk."

I headed north.

Nothing on 91st Street seemed different from the day before. So I parked in the driveway and walked to the Morgasons' front door.

I rang the bell.

When nobody answered the bell, I knocked.

When nobody answered the knock, I walked around the house to look for signs of life.

Checking out a house like that isn't as easy as it sounds. You've got to make sure you don't fall into the swimming pool.

But I saw and heard nothing that was animate.

My deductive Go-for-It Detective mind decided that, perhaps, nobody was at home.

I felt a sudden impulse to break in. I had an intuition that I would find Mrs. Morgason's body.

It was a strong sensation.

I walked to a window where I couldn't be seen from the road.

I looked at it carefully.

I walked away again.

The window was connected to a security system and the risk of my falling into the hands of the police again canceled all impulses.

I got back in my car and drove to West 14th Street.

Suppose her body was in there. What would I do with it?

54

A WOMAN OF ABOUT SIXTY, with a broad friendly face, opened the door.

"Mrs. Hawk?"

"Why, yes."

"My name is Albert Samson."

"Do I know you, Mr. Samson?"

"No, ma'am. But I know Mrs. Morgason and I think you might be able to help me with one or two things I'm trying to do."

"You know Mrs. Morgason?"

"That's right."

"I don't recall seeing you up at the house."

"I've only been in the house once. But I've heard about you."

"Oh yes?" She was not displeased, but at the same time she assessed me. "You wouldn't be trying to sell me something, now, would you?" She looked at the picture I was carrying.

"No ma'am. But one of the things I'd like you to do is look at this drawing."

"Uh-huh. Well, I guess maybe you better come in while I find my glasses."

I followed her and she left me in a living room that was filled with memorabilia. There were small items everywhere, all set up to be seen, to be shown.

There were dozens of pictures. On a prominent shelf next to the mantel I saw large photographs of Mrs. Morgason, of Sick and of many other white people.

When Mrs. Hawk returned with her glasses I said, "I see you've got some nice pictures of Mrs. Morgason and her family."

"They've been so good to me, over the years, those folks," Mrs. Hawk said. "That's all the family, those. I worked for Mrs. Morgason's momma and poppa—that's Mr. and Mrs. Overmeyer there. Oh, Mrs. Overmeyer, she was a fine, fine woman."

"I was told that you've worked for the family for a long time."

"Yessir, I have. More than thirty-two years and that is a long time. And they've been so good to me and my girl, and I'm not ashamed to say it."

"Nice people," I said.

"More than nice. Take Mrs. Overmeyer. She found I didn't read real well. Fact was I didn't read at all. Day after day, she taught me. Reading, writing, talking. Always something to help me improve myself. I can't tell you how much I enjoyed that. Then little Kathryn, that's Mrs. Morgason, she sent my girl to secretarial school, to help my girl get some personal problems sorted out."

"Your daughter is Louanne?"

"Why yes."

"Is Louanne here?"

"Now, why are you asking that?"

"As well as talking to you, I'd like a few words with her."

Mrs. Hawk's forehead creased and she said, "Mister, what is this all about?"

"I am a private detective, Mrs. Hawk." I took out my license card and passed it to her. She put on her glasses and looked back and forth between me and the photograph.

"This you?"

"It sure is. And what I am doing is getting together some information about a man named Cecil Redman."

"Oh," Mrs. Hawk said. "Him."

"It's not that he is in trouble, but I have a client who asked me to check him out and I understand that Louanne is married to Mr. Redman."

Mrs. Hawk was silent for a moment. Then she said, "My momma taught me, if you can't say nothing nice about a body, then don't you say nothing at all."

"Did they ever divorce, Mrs. Hawk?"

"No, but Louanne works in an office full of lawyers, so maybe she's doing something about that now."

"Which office is that?"

"It's called Law In Action. It's out east on 30th Street and it helps poor folks with their rights. They have employed people, like Louanne, but the idea is that a number of downtown lawyers devote time each week to helping needy folks."

"It sounds like a worthwhile place."

"Yessir," Mrs. Hawk said. "It sure is."

"Would Louanne be there today?"

"She's there every day."

"Except maybe when you're sick and she fills in for you at Mrs. Morgason's."

"She's a good girl, my Louanne. She had a wild spell when she was young, but she came through that and she's a real good girl now."

I nodded acceptance of that as a fact. Then I said,"Mrs. Hawk, do you mind if I ask whether you're feeling unwell today?"

"Why do you ask that?"

"Aren't you usually up at Mrs. Morgason's by now?"

"Ah, I see. Yessir, usually I am. Only this morning Mrs. Morgason called me to say not to mind going in today. She's away from home and didn't have a chance to leave me a list of things to do."

"She called you this morning?"

"Yessir, she did."

"What time was that?"

"About a quarter to six."

"Isn't that a little early?"

"She knows I'm always up by five."

"Is it unusual for her to tell you not to come in?"

"It doesn't happen often, but it's like her to be considerate and she won't take it off my money. She'll go and pay me anyhow, 'cause that's the way she is. Did I tell you, she sent my Louanne to school?"

"Secretarial school."

"Yessir, that's right. It's a fact and it changed my little girl's whole life."

"Mrs. Hawk, would you . . . ?" I held up Bobbie Lee's drawing.

She took it to the window to get better light. "Not much face on this picture."

"The person remembered the dress better than the face."

"It's good of the dress. Course without that big old spot. I worked for hours getting that grease and stain off."

"You know the dress?"

"Course I do." She looked at me. "Is that something you want me to talk about?"

"I would like to know about the dress, yes."

"Well, Mrs. Morgason had a party because Mr. Morgason just opened his new business. They had a lot of people and they had a guitar player and I don't know what all."

"Uh-huh."

"Most days I come away from the house between two and three, but when Mrs. Morgason entertains, well, I know it's hard on her so I like to stay on to help."

"I see."

"And there was the strangest man at this party. He was talking and talking about I don't know what all and they couldn't get a word in edgeways. Well, he started waving his arms around and I just knew something was going to happen, and sure enough it did. He knocked over a drink of red wine on this lady he was with. And then, when he was trying to clean her up, he pulled a whole table of food down on her. A whole table! Honestly, I don't know what that man thought he was doing. Maybe he thought the tablecloth was a napkin or something, only when he pulled at it all the plates of salad and cold meat and mustard and butter piled on the lady and this dress. A lot of the folks laughed but the lady, she was so angry!"

I nodded and couldn't help but smile at the image of Quentin Quayle in action.

"The lady, she out-and-out screamed at this man to leave her alone and she was saying things about how much this dress cost and I don't know what all. Mrs. Morgason, she took the lady off to the bathroom and she gave her this piece of Indian cloth—I mean Indian like over in India—and the lady put it on to wear. Wrapped it all around, you know? And then this lady that was so angry, she came back and acted like she was having the time of her life. It was like she was a whole different person."

"Mrs. Hawk, do you remember what happened to the dress?"

She hesitated. "Mrs. Morgason gave it to me."

"To you?"

"She said the lady told her she never wanted to see it again. So Mrs. Morgason, she asked if I wanted it and I did."

"Do you have the dress now?"

"No sir. I cleaned it up and gave it to Louanne."

I raised Bobbie Lee's picture again. "And this is the dress?"

"Oh yes."

"Mrs. Hawk, could this be a drawing of Louanne?"

"Louanne? My Louanne?"

"Yes, ma'am."

"No sir, no way, no how."

"Oh."

"For a start, the girl in that picture's got gloves. My Louanne doesn't wear gloves. She doesn't even own gloves."

"O.K."

"And that dress wouldn't fit her. It took a gal taller and thinner."

"O.K."

"And this girl in the picture, she's too dark-complected to

be Louanne. Not saying Louanne's got airs about her color, but my Louanne's nowhere near so dark-skinned as this gal." She handed the picture back to me. "No sir. Not Louanne."

"But if the dress was the wrong size for her, why did your daughter want it."

"She said, 'Momma, I know the perfect person for that dress.'"

I WAS CLOSING IN ON HER. I could feel it.

Nothing could stop me.

I was slowed down by two guys arguing in the middle of the street about a broken taillight. But I couldn't be stopped.

On the way to East 30th Street I did consider calling Miller.

I *was* closing in on the Ohio Street bomber, after all. I might be in danger.

Calm down, calm down. What you're closing in on is Louanne Hawk Redman, who knows the woman in the picture. But Louanne might not tell you. Not at first.

No point in getting Miller excited prematurely. Premature excitement can be a problem, for cops. If they have their guns out they might fire too early.

Besides, me bringing the Ohio Street bomber in myself was tastier. I liked the idea of that a lot, after the pressure I'd endured. Miller might have his ambition, but I had my pride.

And there was the advertising potential: Albert Samson, scourge of Indianapolis terrorism. Think what Frank could make of that.

*   *   *

Law In Action was a storefront near the corner of Tacoma. Its window was papered at eye level with posters describing the services it could provide.

I didn't read about them. I walked right in.

Just inside the door there was a desk. The woman at it was sorting through a pile of papers.

My eyes were drawn to her hands. On the backs there were large pigmentless areas, perhaps scar tissue. The result was white spots on otherwise dark brown skin.

I watched her.

After a few moments she looked up. She dropped her hands to her sides and said, "Can I help you?"

It was her.

Her.

The woman in the picture.

"I . . . I . . . I . . ."

She rose. She pushed her chair clear with the back of her thighs. Holding her hands out of sight, she moved around the desk.

I couldn't breathe. I looked for some support. I found plastic chairs placed just inside the door. I sat.

She came to stand before me.

I looked away as she got close. I fought for breath, for control.

The woman took Bobbie Lee's drawing from me.

When I looked up at her again, she was staring at it.

Though I heard a voice from elsewhere in the room, I didn't register what it said.

But Picture Woman said, "It's O.K., Louie. This man and I have a little personal business to discuss. We're going to use the interview room. Get my phone, O.K.?"

She leaned forward and took one of my hands. "This way," she said.

56

THE INTERVIEW ROOM WAS windowless and airless, but soundproof. There were even acoustic tiles on the door.

It was furnished with a coffee table and four vinyl-upholstered chairs. On the table there was a fan and Picture Woman turned it on after she closed the door.

The short walk had cleared my head a little.

But the effect of the woman on me was still intense. There was something physical about her I couldn't cope with. And that was all wrong. *I* ought to be in charge here. She had stolen the bomb and I had tracked her down. I should be on a lap of honor, taking the cheers and the flowers and the women.

In fact I was struggling to find breath enough for words. We stood next to the coffee table.

She held up Bobbie Lee's drawing. "That's a great dress, isn't it? I just love it."

I went for "Yes," but didn't get it out quickly enough because she dropped the picture on the table and said, "How did you get from this to me? Was it the gloves?"

She lowered herself into one of the chairs.

Carefully, I sat down across from her. I stayed on the edge. I was trying to get my control back.

But for the moment all I could think of was the warmth of her touch as she led me to the room.

I said nothing.

She held both her hands up so I could see the spots on them clearly. "It's a disease, called vitiligo," she said. "I'm not really self-conscious, but it bothers other people. They think they're going to catch it. So when I go out and don't want to have to explain, I wear gloves." She dropped her hands again. "Hey, aren't you ever going to say anything? Don't you at least have to read me my rights?"

"I am not a cop," I said.

"You're not? You're really not?"

"No."

"Oh, thank you, Lord!" She dropped to her knees and leaned on the table as if at prayer. "I figured I'd get along all right in jail, but, Lord, I am truly thankful not to have to prove it."

"I wouldn't celebrate just yet," I said.

She stopped celebrating.

She studied me. She said, "Hey, I wonder if maybe I've been jumping to conclusions. So you have a picture of me in a dress. So what?"

I waited for her to rise from her knees, but she didn't.

I looked at her fingers, touching each other. I suddenly pictured them touching me, running over my skin. They were beautiful.

I fought to remember what I was here for.

I said, "You took a Scum Front bomb from the sixth-floor fire hose closet in the Merchants Bank Building."

"Oh wow!" she said.

I nodded.

Her eyes opened wider, as if to encompass me more fully.

I said nothing. Moved nothing.

"Oh wow," she said again.

Then she laughed.

I didn't know why.

She said, "I followed her just for the hell of it. I never for a minute believed she *was* Scum Front. I mean, you're all suppose to be crazy foreign *men,* right? But Cecil told Louanne about Mrs. Morgason and these other women buying suitcases of stuff from Claude Williams. Well, Claude sells guns, and after a while I got to thinking, 'What if . . .' *What if?* So I followed her a few times, just to find out if it was *possible.*

"And," I said, "it was."

"When I actually found the bomb, I couldn't believe it!" She clapped her hands. "And then I thought, man, I could take that bomb and put it *anywhere.* Someplace it would mean something. And so I did! I took it! It was the most exciting thing ever happened to me."

She stopped.

I waited.

She said, "You have the loveliest eyes, you know that? All bright."

"What?"

"I never had any power of my own before. And then all of a sudden I had a bomb. It's a hell of a turn-on."

I said, "How did you decide where to use it?"

"By carrying it around," she said easily. "Seeing where it felt comfortable."

"You carried a bomb around the city?"

"It was fun, thinking how crazy people would go if they knew." She rested her head on the table. "It's the way I work," she said lazily. "I need to try things out before I know how they're going to feel. Only no place I took it to ever felt right."

"But you always planned to set it off?"

She sat up. "Oh yeah. I know that's not how you see it, but I just can't get worked up about dirty water when there are homeless people sleeping on steam grates to keep warm. And I'm sorry , I just don't see the point leaving a bomb in a bank and not making any boom."

The words coming out of her mouth began to quell the uprising I had felt elsewhere.

"*Then* I thought of the perfect place."

"Oh?"

"What is Indianapolis? What's the symbol of the city? The 500-mile race, right? So I thought, what's the rush? Wait till the night before the 500 and blow up part of the track. And that's what really felt right."

"So," I said, "why did you change your mind?"

She looked surprised. "I didn't."

"Come off it, lady. A building on Ohio Street got blown up last night and a guy got hurt."

"Yeah," she said. "I heard about that." Then, "Hey, you don't think that was me, do you?"

"Who else?"

"Hey, I wouldn't *hurt* anybody. Not people."

"But . . ."

She said, "My bomb's in my desk."

"What?"

"Or rather, your bomb. That's what you're here for, isn't it? You're part of the Scum Front and you've come to get your bomb back. Right?"

I LEFT LAW IN ACTION carrying a bomb in a plastic L. S. Ayres shopping bag.

I shook as I walked.

I carried the bag to the passenger side of my car and I put it inside on the floor.

I closed the door carefully.

I walked around the car to the driver's side. I steadied myself on the hood. I slid behind the wheel and put the key in the ignition.

Then I tried to think what the hell I was doing.

All I knew was that I was in no shape to do anything.

I realized Bobbie Lee's drawing was still in the LIA office. But I did not go back to get it.

The woman inside scared me. She did things solely because she felt like it. That was another planet in my mind, but in her presence my body risked becoming alien.

I shook myself. There was a persistent tingle in my spine.

It was dangerous even to look at the LIA window.

I moved to start the car. But that triggered a flash of fear: would starting the car set the bomb off?

I didn't see why it should.

But reason did not hold its usual sway.

I folded my arms across the steering wheel and rested my ailing head.

I didn't want to be where I was, but the effort to go anywhere else was too great.

My brain was in the middle of a neurological oil change. All the worn-out gunge had been drained, but nothing new had replaced it. Obviously I had to wait before I started to think again.

So I rested.

I laughed at myself, for using my car as a place of refuge. The symbol of twentieth-century America, the car.

But everybody needs to escape sometimes, so what was the problem about that? Problems are my problem. Everything is a problem. Even the basic things. A place to live.

How can it be so hard to lead a quiet life? One where what I do next is not always a burning issue. It must be possible to lead a life without danger. That was the thing about the last few days. *Danger.* Bombers and jailers and . . . dangerous women.

Mom learning to shoot guns.

The only dangers in a real person's life should be . . . should be drunk drivers and cancer and kids being driven places by other kids and nuclear bombs and AIDS from blood transfusions. Who needs any of the rest of it?

Maybe what I should do is quit this ridiculous private eye stuff. There must be some sort of job around for me. A job with a boss. A nice bossy boss to tell me what to do and when. A job that finishes at a specific time of day. A job with money. It doesn't matter how much. How little, more like. But at least that way I know where I am.

I may lose a little on *who* I am, but what's so bad about that? Am I so goddamn pleased with who I am? Why haven't I ever seriously considered getting a job?

Why don't I think about the things I never think about?

What kind of lunatic am I? My private eyeing isn't going

well, so what do I do? I turn my life upside down to try to do more of it! I "go for it." Go for what? Quit, you jerk! Quit! Be normal. Think about normal things.

How long has it been since you saw your daughter? Years! Waiting for her to sort life out? What's the point of that? Go see her. Get yourself on a plane. Your only begotten child, for Christ's sake. Be normal. See your child.

And what about your own life? Your grown-up life. With your growed-up grown-up woman. Do you talk about marriage? No. It's a nonsubject. Well, maybe marriage *should* be a nonsubject. But what about living together?

You get along. How the hell often does that happen in life? Of course she hadn't exactly cleared a closet for you. But you could ask. Why don't you? Why haven't you? Just because she'll probably say no? What kind of reason is that?

Oh, Samson, you're one of these guys who lives with his nose against the window. Look at life, but don't touch. Look through the window, watch the dolly dance. Whish. Slide. Or how about tap? Tap, tap, shuffle, tap. Huh, funny. Next thing, you're going to take tap dancing lessons. Tap dancing, huh. Tap. *Tap tap tap.*

"Hey. Hey. Mister?"

What?

Tap tap tap.

"C'mon, fella. Hey!"

I raised myself from the steering wheel.

Tap tap tap tap. "Fella! Hey. You all right?"

The window next to me was alive. Pressed up close and rapping on the glass with his knuckle was a policeman.

I rubbed my face.

"Hey fella. You all right? Roll the window down. C'mon!"

I rolled the window down.

"You all right?" He was middle-aged, a patrolman. "I saw you slumped over the wheel. I thought you was in trouble."

"No. I'm O.K."

"Usually guys catch forty winks in their cars, they lie down."

"I didn't have the energy to fall over," I said.

"Do you know you got a low tire back there?"

"What?"

"The tire." He pointed. "It's way down, nearly flat. It needs to be fixed or changed."

"Oh, right," I said. "I remember. I'll do that now."

"O.K.," he said. And he left me.

I started my car.

Doing that reminded me of the bomb again.

I looked at it on the floor beside me.

I looked at the cop as he closed his door and moved his car forward a few feet, waiting for a gap in the traffic. He waved.

A friendly guy. No doubt the kind of man I could drink with, share a few stories with.

I could hardly wait for him to be gone.

I waved back.

Suppose the friendly cop had noticed the bag on the floor and had wanted to know what was in it. Suppose he insisted.

It would have been all over.

I would have been taken downtown. I would have been paraded for the press. Locked in the deepest cell ever conceived. I would have been questioned so intensely I'd beg for the interrogation to be eased back to the third degree. The only kind of lawyer they would let me see would be a blind deaf-mute who spoke nothing but Tzotzil.

Spoke what?

Exactly.

I would have carried the can for the whole thing.

The concept was ridiculous. I was too young to be jailed for life. I was too old to be jailed for life.

I headed for home. To clean up and get my head together.

Then I would take the bomb to Miller.

IN THE FIRST GAS STATION I came to I changed the
leaky tire for the spare.

On the way home I did not exceed the speed limit by so
much as a mile an hour.

I braked whenever I saw a yellow light.

I invited buses to pull out in front of me.

I stopped behind each stop sign, and then edged to the
corner to look for cross-traffic.

When I got to Virginia Avenue I did not park across from the
office. Instead I turned around and left the car down the road,
in front of Peppy's Grill. Peppy's is Mom's major competition.
It's farther away from Fountain Square but it has cold beer to
carry-out.

I locked the . . . bag in the trunk.

But I went to the luncheonette instead of up to my office. It
was pushing one-thirty. What with one regurgitation or another, I was starving.

Policemen are also better faced with high blood sugar levels.

I walked in the door and found Quentin Quayle playing on the pinball machine.

"Oh, Jesus H. Doughnut," I said.

From behind the counter, Norman said, "Mustard or relish with that?"

Poet won a replay. I heard him say, "Oh, splendid."

I approached the counter. "Where's my mother?" I asked Norman.

"She went to see her lawyer. I got a chicken steak left."

"What's she doing at the lawyer?"

"Making her will."

"Oh, yeah?"

"Everybody should make a will. It saves all kinds of trouble later on."

"You made yours?" I asked.

Beside me a pear-shaped man in a sweat-stained Stetson said, "Hem."

Norman said to me, "While you read the menu I'll look after this paying customer."

Read the menu! I damn well painted it and hung it on the wall.

Quayle won another replay.

The Stetson pear ordered the steak.

I considered a theatrical exit and going down the street to eat at Peppy's.

But eating in a place like that could be risky. To my certain knowledge there are sometimes bombs in the trunks of cars parked outside Peppy's.

I bent over the counter and chuckled to myself.

I continued to be amused as I went behind the counter to pour myself a cup of coffee.

I was laughing as I carried it toward the pinball machine. I spilled some into the saucer. I was in danger of working myself up to a genuine giggle fit.

"Oh dear," I said. "Oh dear."

I set my coffee on the table closest to Quayle's action and asked, "What the hell are you doing here, Poet?"

"Wait," Quayle told me. "I'm winning replays!"

I went back to the counter. As I passed Norman I said, "BLT, no mayo, on rye and a bowl of chili." He made no acknowledgment that he had heard me.

I went to the doorway that leads into the house. There I flipped one of several electrical switches, waited a moment and flipped it back.

I returned to the table with my cup on it and sat down.

Quentin Quayle was cursing and hitting the machine.

"Problem?" I asked.

"I couldn't put a flipper wrong and then the damn thing suddenly went off."

"You must have tilted," I said.

"Rubbish!"

"Did all the lights go off and then come back on again?"

"Yeah."

"Tilt," I said. "Gotta be. Come here a minute, Poet. Take a seat."

He came and sat.

I moved my chair closer to his. I beckoned to him to listen up. I said in a loud whisper, "What the fuck are you doing here?"

But as he often did, he answered his own interrogator. "I didn't see you drive up." He looked out the window. "Where's your car?"

"Poet, answer my question or you're a dead man."

He leaned back and raised his eyebrows and inhaled. "Well, Albert, old chum, I hate to do this to you, but I'm taking you off the case."

"What case?"

"Surveillance of Charlotte. No hard feelings, I hope, but I want my money back."

"What money?"

"I gave you a thousand dollars. There must be some left."

I considered. Probably there was. I said, "O.K. When I get a chance I'll draw up your bill and give you your change."

"I'd like it now."

"Well, you can't have it now."

"Why not?"

"Because," I said with British understatement, "I've got more important things to do than work on your account."

He pouted for a moment.

"Besides," I said, "Why all of a sudden don't you want Charlotte Vivien followed anymore? Is she marrying somebody else?"

"She did see a man last night," Quayle said in a lowered voice. "We followed her to this incredibly scruffy bar and she met someone there."

"Oh yeah?"

"Ugly," Quayle said. "And old."

I looked surprised.

"I didn't see him myself, of course, but Bobbie Lee described the guy to me."

"Oh," I said.

"And he was dirty too, this ugly old man."

"Hard to imagine what Mrs. Vivien's interest in someone like that could be."

"I could hardly believe it. She's always seemed so fastidious."

"Yes," I said.

"She's a wonderful woman," Quayle said.

"So you keep saying."

"Not Charlotte."

"What?"

"Bobbie Lee," he said. And he sighed.

I just stared at him

"She's so . . . so competent and sure. Of course she's not educated to a high standard. Your system here is so punitive to people without financial resources. But she's genuinely intelligent and earthily perceptive in a way that the culture vultures like Charlotte could never be."

I sipped from my coffee.

"And it is incredible the way she's supported little Bill, Nora and Glenn."

"Who?"

"The handicapped triplets. And now her dementing mother as well. Bobbie's life story is a distillation of the attractive face of feminism. She's so spunky and quick and strong."

"And imaginative."

"And, of course, she's got that great body and those beautiful chocolate-brown eyes."

"She has?"

"Oh yes," he said. "I'm a poet. I notice things like that."

"Sounds like you're in love again, Poet."

"Albert," he said, "I am."

"And tell me, do you think the lady returns your feelings?"

"I think," he said, looking me in the eye, "that she thinks I am less of a jackass than she originally thought."

Self-awareness now? For once I was impressed.

"Well," I said. "Good luck to you."

Norman arrived with my BLT and chili. He said, "These both for you, Albie, or is one for your date?"

I rose and said, "Norman Tubbs. Quentin Quayle. You guys ought to get acquainted. I think you have a lot in common."

Poet said, "How do you do?"

Norman said, "You're not related to S. Quentin Quail of the Bonafide Oil Company, by any chance."

"You like the Marx Brothers?" Poet asked.

"Love them."

"Me too."

"Hang on," I said. "Will somebody tell me what's going on here?"

Dismissively Norman said, "S. Quentin Quail is the character Groucho played in *Go West*." Then to Poet he said, "Why don't you come over to the counter. Albie can probably just about cut up his food for himself."

And without another word they left me—struck dumb and mouth hanging open.

59

WHEN I FINISHED EATING I made an unnoticed escape
through the house to my office. The new soulmates probably
wouldn't have cared anyway, but I didn't want to take a
chance.

Despite the comfort of a full belly, I was nervous as I
opened the door to my quarters. I let it swing wide before I
went into my bedroom. But there was no one inside and no
obvious sign of a recent visit.

I felt foolish, but I had had a hell of a few days. Nothing
seemed genuinely to surprise me anymore except lack of
surprises.

The observation didn't make enough sense to be poetic.
I considered it, therefore, to be philosophic.

There wasn't even any mail.

There were, however, messages on my answering machine. But before I listened to them I showered and changed
into fresh clothes and became a new man and managed not to
think of bombers for seconds at a stretch.

There were five messages in all.

The first of the day was from Bobbie Lee. She asked me to call and to tell her answering machine to wake her up.

The next three messages were, incredibly, from prospective new clients.

Finally, Frank spoke urgently of the need for eight hundred dollars.

Nothing on the machine was more important than my seeing Miller.

Yet I hesitated.

What I wanted to say to Miller wasn't clear in my head.

I found myself feeling that I shouldn't rush to the police just yet.

And one reason for delaying was the image of my little friend Sick.

There was no justification, philosophic or poetic, for Kathryn Morgason doing what she had done. But in a world as barbarous and cruel as this one, where the suffering inflicted for personal gain is immeasurable, I did not believe that Kathryn Morgason had done enough to deserve having the key thrown away.

Judge Samson was it now?

Well, why not? Judge Samson was at least as "wise" as any other judge.

But I also hesitated to spill my guts to Miller because I did not feel that I understood enough about what had happened and why.

And what responsible judge would make a decision without all the facts?

Yet there was a bomb in my car.

I don't make life easy for myself.

I sat for a while at my desk. I tried to begin a list. Things I could do. Options. But before long I found myself doodling. Wavy lines became hands. The hands acquired spots. The spots began to take erotic forms.

Then the telephone rang.

As I picked it up I realized that I shouldn't have. It could be Miller. It should be Miller.

I said, "You have reached the Albert Samson Investigative Services Agency. Mr. Samson cannot come to the telephone right now but if you will leave your name and tel—"

"Bull *shit*," Bobbie Lee said.

"Ah."

"I wanted to let you know that I am awake and I'm ready to drive over in case you are the slightest bit interested in a pretty unusual surveillance report. But, gee, Mr. Samson, sir, if you are too important these days to get reports from—"

"I'm sorry," I said. "I was afraid you were the police."

After a pause she said, "I didn't think you ran that kind of operation."

"I don't," I said. "It's a complicated story. But come to the office, please. I'll be here."

"I don't want to get mixed up with the police. They take too goddamn much time."

"You won't. In fact," I said, improvising, "I have more work for you." I looked at the list of client calls on my pad. Well, why not? "A lot more work."

She thought about that.

"But watch yourself when you get here. Quentin Quayle is downstairs."

"You know, Albert," she said, "that guy isn't quite the jackass you think he is."

Bobbie Lee Leonard look tired. "Late night?" I asked.

"If you've seen Quentin, you know damn well it was," she said.

"We didn't talk about it."

She smiled. "Hasn't he got the cutest way of saying things?"

"It's what he says I have the problem with."

"Well, you want this report or not?"

"I do."

She took a notebook from her handbag. "On paper it's only a list of where and when. I haven't had a chance to write it up fancy and make the client think he's got his money's worth."

"He thinks he got his money's worth all right."

"So verbal is all right?"

"And simple. I just want to know what happened."

"Well, the Vivien woman went out in the early evening and she headed downtown, only she stopped at a public phone on the way and made a call."

"O.K."

"Then she went to a little bar out East Washington and met this man."

"Yeah. I've heard about the 'scruffy' bar and the ugly, dirty old man with halitosis, dandruff and a patch over one eye."

"I guess I forgot to mention he didn't wear no underwear and only had the one ball."

"Yeah yeah."

"But I don't understand why you hire me to follow somebody and don't tell me you are going to meet her yourself."

"I didn't know."

"No?"

"Quentin identified the dress in the picture you drew as one of Mrs. Vivien's. So after you left I called her and she agreed to meet me."

"So you were on another case? The picture case?"

"Yeah. So where did Mrs. Vivien go after she left the bar?"

"She stopped at another phone booth and this time she made two calls, not one."

"To what numbers?"

"You wish," Bobbie Lee said.

"And then?"

"Then," she said, "she went to a motel out Washington Street."

"A motel?"

"Just the other side of 465. She went into reception and was there for a few minutes and came out with some keys."

"Quentin must have been having a fit."

"He didn't say."

"And once Mrs. Vivien had her keys?"

"She drove away. And she went to a shopping center and found another phone and made two more calls."

"Uh-huh."

"And then she went into a supermarket."

"Hang on."

"And bought a bag of groceries and about ten o'clock she went back to the motel and went into a room."

"Alone?"

"The room was dark when she went in. Lights came on as she closed the door."

"O.K."

"We parked where we could see pretty good but nothing happened. Once she had been in there for a while I went to reception and talked to the clerk. It cost you money, but I found out that Mrs. Vivien booked three rooms, all in a row. And the one she'd gone into was the middle room."

"Hmmm."

"Then people started arriving. First a woman, in a BMW. Then two more together, in a Ford."

"Women?"

"Yeah. All white. First one was maybe five feet tall and she moved well, you know? Athletically. In her thirties I'd guess, but I didn't get a good look. She wore a long jacket and a scarf. The other two, one was older and one was younger. Both about five four or five. They had long jackets on too, and scarves. The two together had a couple of suitcases."

I just sat.

"This stuff mean something to you?"

"I can't quite believe it but it does."

"Do I get to ask what?"

I said nothing.

"I thought not," she said. "That's one of the reasons I've got time for Quentin. He may not say it in words, but you always know where you are with him."

I shrugged.

"Is something wrong?"

I said, "Did you get the plate numbers?"

"Of course."

"Bobbie Lee, did you put them through to get the owners?"

She grinned. Her tongue played in the gap between her teeth. "Sure did, boss." She flipped a page in her notebook. "You want the list?"

I nodded.

"BMW is registered to a guy named Morgason."

"And the Ford?"

"Lillian Ray. You want the addresses?"

"Not now. Finish the report."

The page came back. But instead of beginning again she said, "You all right?"

"Great."

"You look like shit."

I said nothing.

"Well, all these women went to the room Mrs. Vivien was in."

"What time did the last two get there?"

"Ten past eleven."

"And then?"

"Quentin and I waited outside till five-fifteen."

"Nobody came out?"

"Nobody. And the lights stayed on."

"Nobody else went in?"

"I would have said."

"Bobbie Lee, might they still be there now?"

60

SOMEBODY LESS TIRED THAN I was might have gotten it earlier.

When I talked to them in the phone booth Monday night, the Scummies had been furious. They had called me "treacherous" and referred to my "cop friends."

I had never figured out why.

But *now* I knew. Monday was the first night Bobbie Lee followed Charlotte Vivien. It was also the night that Quentin Quayle followed her. Vivien had spotted Quayle and taken tire-squealing evasive action to shake him. But she had thought she was shaking a cop and for a cop to be tailing her meant that I must have betrayed them.

Later that night I displayed the hanky in my window. I wanted to talk.

So did they. And everything they had had to say was angry.

If I'd only managed to associate their unexpected anger with the shaken tail, I would have known then that Charlotte Vivien was one of them. The Gorilla. The one who hadn't ever spoken in my presence.

Oh God! My woman and Miller had both asked the key question: why did the Scum Front come to me in the first place? Why *me*?

I had asked it too and been told it was because I worked alone. But that wasn't enough. No. The Scum Front came to me because, when they decided to hire someone to look for their missing bomb, Charlotte Vivien was able to say that she already knew a private detective. One who could be paid to do just about anything. Even a goddamn murder dinner party.

I picked up the phone.

Bobbie Lee watched.

I dialed Charlotte Vivien's number. Loring answered. I asked for Mrs. Vivien. I was told she was not at home. I asked when she was expected. He said he didn't know.

Then, for what felt like the hundredth time that day, I dialed Kathryn Morgason. But this time I was afraid that she *would* answer.

She didn't.

When I hung up, Bobbie Lee said quietly, "You could have called the motel to see if they checked out."

I nodded. "If I'd thought of it."

She studied me. "This is something serious."

"Yes," I said. Then, "I've got to go there."

"You want me to come?"

I was surprised at the offer.

But pleased.

"I still won't be able to tell you what it's all about."

"O.K.," she said easily. "I'll try to figure it out as I go along. Ain't nothing so intriguing as a little mystery."

"If you say so."

"Correct me if I'm wrong," she said, "but I get the feeling you'd trade the intrigue for a little sleep."

"Honestly," I said, "I no longer really know what I'm doing."

"Is that supposed to be a news flash?"

"I guess not."

"One car or two?"

I was sorely tempted to go in her Rabbit. It was unlikely to have a bomb in it.

But it wouldn't be "socially responsible" to leave my car.
Or to ask her to ride in it. "Two," I said.

I followed as she led to the motel. She drove quickly.

I had to concentrate to keep up.

But not too hard to wonder whether Bobbie Lee Leonard
carried a gun.

By the time we got there I didn't want to ask. I wouldn't
like the answer either way.

She parked near the end of one group of motel rooms.

There was a space next to her but I passed it. I drove my
bomb as far away from her car as I could.

She stood by her Rabbit and watched as I walked back
across the lot.

"Problem?" she asked.

"No."

I slipped into her passenger seat and she got back in too.
Shaking her head. But she said, "Their cars are still here."

So this was it. I had them together.

But what was I going to do with them?

"Where?" I asked.

She pointed them out. "And the room is up there, second
from the end. Forty-seven."

We were almost directly in front of it.

"I want you to move the car," I said.

"What?"

I looked for a place away from the room and away from
my car. "Over there," I said. I pointed.

"Why?"

"I'm afraid they might see you here."

"But they don't know me."

I looked at her.

She said, "Yes, boss," and started the engine.

"Back into the space, so you can see the room door."

"So what happens now?" she asked when we were settled
again.

"I go up and knock, I guess."

"And if they won't let you in?"

"I'll huff and I'll puff and I'll blow the door down."

Or put a note under it saying if they didn't open up I'd go to the police. The principle was the same.

"Nervous, huh?" Bobbie Lee said.

"Yeah."

"Look, let me go to reception and try to get a key."

"A key? How the hell you going to do that?"

"Ah," she said, "I'll only show you my little secrets if you'll show me yours."

I didn't know what to say.

"You want me to try?"

If I had a key I could surprise them.

Was that good? Or would that make something go bang? Or would knocking on the door make something go bang?

"Go on," I said.

She went.

I sat in the car and fidgeted.

I worried about the suitcases.

I knew what the Scum Front carried in suitcases.

What if they were making new bombs? What if they were about to blow themselves up in a spectacular final gesture?

Was there any reason to think they'd do that?

Well, I would go in anyway. No way was I going to get this close and back off.

Then I got worried because I hadn't made a will.

So I wrote one, on a piece of notebook paper.

Everything to my only child except my books. Those to my woman friend. And a wish for good luck to Miller. My mother as executor without bond. No eight hundred dollars to Frank.

Bobbie Lee came back grinning the most beguiling gap-toothed grin I had ever seen. She dropped onto the seat and jingled a key in front of me.

"That was quick," I said.

"Shows I was dealing with a man," she said.

I began to speak but she interrupted. "Clerk last night

complained he was having to do double shifts. So it was the same guy. He likes money."

"I want you to witness something."

"What are you talking about?"

I signed the will and passed it to her.

But even that didn't wipe the smile. "Give me the pen," she said, and wrote her name by mine. "You are just about the nuttiest fella I ever worked for."

"Today I can believe that," I said.

"So," she said, "you're going into the room. You want me to come too?"

"No."

"What do you want me to do?"

"Call the cops if I don't come out, I guess."

"After how long?"

"I don't know. Use your judgment, but give me some time."

"I take it you figure these women are dangerous."

"I don't think they are, but they might be."

"Are you sure you want to do whatever it is you're doing?"

"No. But I'm sure I don't want not to do it."

"If you were someone else," she said, "I'd ask what that was supposed to mean. When you going?"

"Now," I said. I got out of the car.

Room 47 was up a slight incline from the parking lot. I walked straight to the sidewalk in front of the door.

I felt naked. It wasn't because I didn't have a gun. It was because I didn't have any ideas.

I was also frightened.

I approached the door and listened.

Nothing.

I tried to see in the window but the curtains were closed tight.

I turned back to Bobbie Lee. She was watching impassively.

I moved to the door and slid the key into the lock. I gave it a wiggle. The door opened.

I eased myself inside.

The air in the closed room smelled stale.

I found the light switch.

I turned it on.

They were all there. All four of them.

They lay two each on the twin beds, but they were dressed in street clothes.

They were motionless.

They were silent.

They were dead.

I BACKED OUT OF THE ROOM and pulled the door closed behind me. I gasped for fresh air.

It was right for the people inside room 47 to feel guilt for what they had done. They needed to suffer for the anxiety their "bombs" had caused.

But they did not need to be dead.

No.

No. That was *wrong*.

The threat to them, their lives, was not great enough for that.

The threat to them was me.

I leaned against the wall by the door. Then I slid down it and sat on the walk.

I heard a sound from the parking lot. Bobbie Lee had opened the door of her car.

She saw that I had seen her. She stopped.

I shook my head.

No. It was wrong.

She got back in the car. To wait. To see what I would do.

I realized I should do something.

I rolled to my knees. I got to my feet.

What should I do? Ambulance? Police?

Go back in first, I supposed.

I turned to the door.

I took a breath.

I grasped the doorknob.

It turned as I touched it.

I jumped back. I couldn't speak.

The door opened and Charlotte Vivien stood in front of me.

"You," she said sleepily. "I suppose I should have known that it had to be the bad penny."

62

WE SPENT MORE THAN AN hour together, the combined membership of the Scum Front and I. I became acquainted with Lillian Ray and her daughter, Rachel: the Bear and "Kate King." I heard how it all started. I heard how the name came from the woman who tried to kill Andy Warhol on behalf of the Society to Cut Up Men, SCUM, and how they thought the name was funny. I heard how they had met last night to talk everything through. I heard how they had decided to give it all up. The problem was working out how. They made me coffee.

Not evil people. Innocents of a kind. People who could attend a meeting and hear a speaker ask, "What are *you* doing about the environment?" and take it seriously, personally. "At first I just made sure to use ozone-friendly hair spray," Kathryn Morgason told me. "We all did."

"And unleaded gas," Lillian Ray said. "But it was all so small. So trivial. What was the point when General Motors and General Electric and the generals at the Pentagon weren't making the same effort?"

"For me it was soap," Charlotte Vivien said.

"That's right," Lillian Ray said. "You buy vegetable oil soap to save the whales but the supermarket is still stacked with the other kind. It makes you feel so powerless."

"And then," Charlotte Vivien said, "you begin to ask yourself where the real power in society is."

"It isn't people working alone," Kathryn Morgason said.

"You have to find each other," Lillian Ray said. "You have to think it through. You have to be able to work out plans. You'll never have power yourself, but if you work it out right you might be able to make the people with the power do something."

The turning point was when Rachel Ray came home from high school one day with a copy of *Poor Man's James Bond*. Classmates had been selling them via a computer notice board.

Bond is a bomb-making book, like *The Anarchist's Cookbook* in the sixties. Except that *Bond* even gives instructions for putting together a nuclear bomb.

The police had broken up the high school enterprise. But not before "Kate King" got her copy.

Then, when her mother next talked about her friends, Rachel Ray said, "I've got something you'll be interested in, Mother."

Mother had looked at the *Bond*. "Bombs?"

"I thought you said you guys wanted to *do* something."

So Rachel joined the "group" and they had ended up doing something.

Kathryn Morgason brought media know-how. She'd been a copywriter before she married her television magnate.

Lillian Ray had the contacts that led to an illicit dynamite supplier. She was an assistant professor of sociology.

And Charlotte Vivien had the money. And the driving energy. She wanted to spend both on something more significant than giving great parties and sponsoring poets in residence.

And between them they had scared the shit out of a city.

"But we never once considered that someone might pick up one of our bombs and *use* it," Lillian Ray said.

There was a chorus of agreement.

"Nobody did use it," I said.

"What?"

"Wait here."

Bobbie Lee stood by and watched me take the plastic bag from my trunk. She called to me as I headed back to the room, "I can tell from the way you're walking that it's going all right. What's in the bag? Lunch?"

"Yup," I said. But I winked.

Getting their bomb back didn't make them feel better.

That was good.

They didn't deserve to feel better. The atmosphere they created had nerved up the imitators who put a man in the hospital.

But I had made the decision that I had to make. I would not give the police their names.

"So," I said, "what do you people plan to *do* to make amends?"

63

WHEN I CLOSED THE TRUNK I got in the car and faced
Bobbie Lee. I said, "You still in this?"

"It's borderline. The excitement of doing nothing night
and day is almost more than I can bear."

"If everything goes all right," I said, "I'll be able to give
you a lot of work soon."

"So you keep promising."

"We might even work out some kind of partnership or
something."

"You get the jobs and I do them? You know what's going
on and I don't? You go into the motel and I sit outside?
Thanks, fella, but I know all about partnerships like that."

She followed me to College Avenue. Cecil Redman's "flat-
back" truck was not outside his house.

We parked in front of the house next door. The house I
loved, with its veranda and its gables and its decaying arch.

Bobbie Lee watched as I went to my trunk and took out
two suitcases and a plastic bag.

I carried everything to the house.

The door was locked, but that was no problem. I walked in through the wall.

The idea was to dump the bomb makings somewhere anonymous, as if the Scum Front had done it.

I found myself in the living room. Artistically, I favored a dump in the fireplace. It was big enough, and the remains of the mantelpiece showed that it had been a beautiful feature.

But there was a massive hole in the floor in front of it and the signs of rot nearby convinced me to take a more practical course.

There was a closet in the room. I put the suitcases and the bag in that.

I spent a long time dealing with possible fingerprints.

Then I leaned the closet door against the frame from which it once had swung.

"I want you to watch the house," I told Bobbie Lee.

"Makes a change from watching a motel, I guess," she said.

"Kids play around here sometimes. They shouldn't play with what I left inside."

She said nothing.

"But the cops will be here soon. You can go when they arrive."

"And what building do I sit outside after that?"

"My office," I said. "With any luck I shouldn't be all that long. And I want to talk to you about our future."

"*Our* future?"

Miller was out when I arrived, but his secretary let me wait in his room while she tracked him down.

Captains get comfortable chairs. I leaned back and put my feet up on his blotter.

Miller would not like it when I refused to give him the membership list of the Scum Front.

But I would counter by offering to phone in an anonymous tip-off about where he could find a closet full of explosives. In the closet he would also find a farewell message from the Scummies. "Continuing police pressure," it would say, "has forced us to end our campaign prematurely. We very much regret our contribution to the atmosphere that led OTHERS to injure the Ohio Street night watchman. We oppose physical violence of any kind. We now see that our campaign was misguided, however laudable its aims."

A literary analyst might see that the style of the Farewell Message differed from Early Scum Front.

I didn't think the police would care a lot about that.

I was betting that they would settle for being given the credit for driving the Scum Front out of existence. And recovering the bomb-making stuff would give them something physical to show the press and the public.

I was betting that would be enough. That they wouldn't also insist on a body. Someone to prosecute. Someone to spit at. Not when they still had other, "real" bombers to find. Nuts who had blown up a building on Ohio Street and a man with it. And about them I genuinely knew nothing.

As for the Scummie Wrap-up, surely Miller needn't even "know" who tipped him off.

I might just get out of the whole thing unscathed.

Could that happen? Was it possible even though we were dealing with terrorists here, however dangerless? Wouldn't someone have to pay?

I finally heard footsteps outside.

I took a breath and prepared.

As Miller walked through the door I said, "Come on in, Jerry. Sit down. Get comfy. But I warn you, you're not going to like everything I have to say."

Miller said nothing. He just stood. He looked terrible but before I had a chance to make a crack about it he was roughly pushed aside.

Behind him a man came through the door with a gun in his hand.

I recognized the man from pictures. And from Charlotte Vivien's party, a lifetime ago. He was the Chief of Police.

"Consorting with terrorists, huh, Samson?" he said. "Well, you're not going to like everything I have to say either."

Miller finally spoke. He said, "Sorry, Al. Sorry."

EVENTUALLY THEY GOT tired of listening to me not
answer their questions. They decided to talk in private with
my lawyer. So they left me alone. Locked in a secure cell, but
alone. I was more grateful for the peace than I could say.

Not that anybody asked.

After about an hour the door clanked. I jumped up. I thought
my lawyer was back.

But the door did not open.

I said, "Hello? Hello? Who's there?"

"Chow time," a man outside said.

"Oh."

Nothing happened for a moment. Then a square panel in
the door slid open, about eye high. I saw an eye. The eye was
opened wide and curious. It pressed close to the hole. "So
you're the Scum Front," the man outside my cell said. "What
a disappointment."

On my lawyer's advice, I said nothing.

"I was sure you guys was young, not middle-aged and

pudgy. I thought at least you'd look wild. But you don't look tough or anything."

"What is the time of day, please?"

"Took your watch away, huh?"

"They thought I might hang myself with it."

The eye glanced away. "Quarter past five. You want this food or not?"

"Is there a doughnut?" I felt like someone to talk to.

"A what?"

"Yeah, I'll take the food," I said.

The door clanked again before I finished explaining the nature of life to the chocolate pudding. My spoon was poised for life's punch line.

This time there were two male voices.

One I didn't recognize said, "Only a minute. Jesus, you know what kind of chance I'm taking?"

"I know," the other man said. That voice I knew.

The door opened and Miller came in.

I stood up. We faced each other. Neither of us spoke. Sometimes that's the way people who know each other well talk best.

Then he shrugged and said, "Damn it, Al, you called me. You said you'd done things for the Scum Front. You know what the pressure's been like around here."

"So you told somebody?"

He nodded. "I just had to. I couldn't keep that kind of shit to myself."

"You could have waited," I said. "You could have waited till you heard what I had to say."

But he hadn't waited. That made him just like me. I could have waited to phone him when I thought the Scummies set the bomb off on Ohio Street. But I hadn't waited to check.

"I'll do whatever I can for you, Al. You know that."

He left before I could think of anything else I wanted to say.

* * *

So, Go-for-It Detective, here you are in jail. I hope you like it, 'cause you're going to be here a long time.

I don't know if I agree with that.

Do you honestly expect a suspected member of the Scum Front to get bail?

I'm no member of the Scum Front. The cops know that.

But they're going to want you for a scapegoat, sunshine.

Yeah, maybe.

No maybe about it.

Well, even cops don't always get what they want.

Get real, gumshoe.

I'll get out. I'll trade them for what's in the arched house on College.

Oh yeah?

I've just got to get the timing right.

And meanwhile Bobbie Lee sits outside?

I feel bad about that. But it's nearly six o'clock. She'll have figured out that things didn't go according to plan.

Plan? *Plan?*

Yeah, well . . .

So why not just tell the cops the goddamn names and be done with it? Now, that *would* get you out of here.

But I don't want to tell them the names.

Judge Samson again, is it?

I guess maybe it is. And it's my life. I'm entitled.

So what are you going to do with your life, Judge?

That is not entirely within my control.

What do you *want* to do with your life, Judge?

Ah. That's a hard one. All I know for sure at the moment are the things I don't want.

Such as?

I don't want the Franks and their commercials. I don't want endless messages on an answering machine. I don't want to have to spend sunny afternoons typing up invoices. I don't want to be under pressure and tired all the time.

So it's like your mother said? "We aren't all meant to be successful, son."

I just don't want to be successful as a Go-for-It Private Detective, that's all.

Just as well. If you think you're going to get out of here with a P.I. license, you're crazy.

Hey, give me a break. Get off my case. You want to know what's going to happen to me? You want to know how this will go?

Yeah, tell me.

O.K. What will happen is this. I'll get out on bail in exchange for giving the cops the bomb-making stuff and farewell message. And they'll think they're on a roll. Only the roll will stop there, because I won't play anymore. But while they're huffing and puffing and making my life miserable, another bomb will go off. It'll be obvious it's not the Scum Front. And they'll turn their attention to that because they know full well that chasing bombers who bomb is more important than chasing bombers who don't. And they'll catch the others, and that'll give them people to parade. Meanwhile I'll have all the lawyering that Charlotte Vivien's money can buy. And what the lawyering will buy is time.

Time?

Maybe it will drag on for a couple of years, but the longer it goes, the further out of mind the Scum Front will be. Face it: they never killed anybody and they never blew anything up. And one day Albert Samson will receive a letter saying that all charges have been dropped.

Yeah, O.K. That's possible.

Damn right it's possible.

But tell me this. What will Albert Samson do in the meantime? Because no way do you keep your license.

They'll "suspend" my license. That's what they'll do. They'll suspend it for a long time. And after charges get dropped the lawyers can go to work on getting it back.

But meanwhile?

Maybe Bobbie Lee will run the business.

And Albert Samson lives on the profits? Ho-ho.

I don't know. I don't know.

No way is your woman going to support you.

At least she'll understand.

For a while. But then she'll need you to get off your butt and do *something*.

Well, how about fixing up decaying houses? Making them into places where people could live again? I like the idea of that.

Are we talking about more of Charlotte Vivien's money?

A loan. It would be an investment.

Doesn't that smack of corruption, Judge Samson?

Well, maybe. And maybe I wouldn't be able to stomach it. But then again, maybe I would. I'll need some time to think about all that. And time is suddenly something I have a lot of.